W9-DEZ-064

Smart High School Series

Grade 10

Quadratic Relations

Popular Canada Parents' Club

To Our Valued Customers:

We would like to welcome you to join our Popular Parents' Club Rewards Program. By scanning the QR code above and signing up to become a member of "**Popular Canada Parents' Club**", you will enjoy the following benefits:

- free educational videos of learning tips by Canadian teachers
- our newsletter informing you of our most recent product releases
- promotional codes for exclusive discounts which can be used during your next purchase
- free educational printables
- eligibility to win a quarter end prize for an iPad
- eligibility to win a quarter end prize worth $100 in workbooks
- eligibility to win other gifts

Your Partner in Education,
Popular Book Company (Canada) Limited

ISBN: 978-1-77149-449-6

Smart High School Series – MathSmart Grade 10 (Quadratic Relations) is designed to help students build solid foundations in high-school-level math and excel in key math concepts.

This workbook covers the key concepts of quadratic relations in the Mathematics curriculum, including topics on:

- Factoring Polynomials
- Forms of Quadratic Relations
- Transformation of Parabolas
- Solving Quadratic Equations

This workbook contains four chapters, with each chapter covering a math topic. Different concepts within the topic are each introduced by a "Key Ideas" section and examples are provided to give students an opportunity to consolidate their understanding. The "Try these!" section allows students to ease into the concept with basic skill questions, and is followed by the "Practice" section with questions that gradually increase in difficulty to help students consolidate the concept they have learned. Useful hints are provided to guide students along and help them grasp the essential math concepts. In addition, a handy summary of the concepts learned is included at the end of each chapter along with space for students to make their own notes for quick and easy reference whenever needed.

A quiz at the end of each chapter as well as a final test are provided to recapitulate the concepts and skills students have learned in the book. The questions are classified into four categories to help students evaluate their own learning. Below are the four categories:

- Knowledge and Understanding
- Application
- Communication
- Thinking

This approach to testing practice effectively prepares students for the Math examination in school.

Additionally, the "Math IRL" sections throughout the book demonstrate the use of the investigated math topics in real-life scenarios to help students recognize the ubiquity and function of math in everyday settings. Bonus online resources can also be accessed by scanning the included QR codes.

At the end of this workbook is an answer key that provides thorough solutions with the crucial steps clearly presented to help students develop an understanding of the correct strategies and approaches to arrive at the solutions.

MathSmart Grade 10 (Quadratic Relations) will undoubtedly reinforce students' math skills and strengthen the conceptual foundation needed as a prerequisite for exploring mathematics further in their secondary programs.

Contents

Chapter 1

Operations with Polynomials

1.1 Factoring and Expanding Polynomials

Key Ideas

Polynomials are algebraic expressions that contain one or more terms. In standard form, a polynomial is a sum and/or difference of terms.

A factorable polynomial can be written as a product of its factors. Each factor can have more than one term.

One way to factor a polynomial is by dividing out the GCF (greatest common factor):

❶ Identify the GCF of the terms.
❷ Divide each term by the GCF.

Examples

Factor the polynomials.

$2x + 8$ ← GCF of $2x$ and 8: 2
$= 2(x + 4)$ ← $2x \div 2 = x$ and $8 \div 2 = 4$
↑
GCF

$4x^2 + 12$ ← GCF of $4x^2$ and 12: 4
$= 4(x^2 + 3)$ ← $4x^2 \div 4 = x^2$ and $12 \div 4 = 3$
↑
GCF

$3x^2 + 6x$ ← GCF of $3x^2$ and $6x$: $3x$
$= 3x(x + 2)$ ← $3x^2 \div (3x) = x$ and $6x \div (3x) = 2$
↑
GCF

Determine the GCF of the terms in each polynomial. Then fill in the blanks to factor the polynomial.

Try these!

① $2x + 4$ ← GCF of $2x$ and 4: ☐

$= $ ☐ $(x + 2)$
↑
GCF

② $3x - 9$ ← GCF of $3x$ and 9: ☐

$= $ ☐ $(x - 3)$
↑
GCF

③ $4x - 12$ ← GCF of $4x$ and 12: ☐

$= $ ☐ $(x - $ ☐ $)$
↑
divide 12 by GCF

④ $3x + 6$ ← GCF of $3x$ and 6: ☐

$= $ ☐ $($ ☐ $+ 2)$
↑
divide $3x$ by GCF

⑤ $2x^2 + 10$ ← GCF of $2x^2$ and 10: ☐

$= $ ☐ $($ ☐ $+ $ ☐ $)$

⑥ $5x^2 - 10$ ← GCF of $5x^2$ and 10: ☐

$= $ ☐ $($ ☐ $- $ ☐ $)$

⑦ $3x^2 + 9x$ ← GCF of $3x^2$ and $9x$: ☐

$= $ ☐ $($ ☐ $+ $ ☐ $)$

⑧ $3x^2 - 6x$ ← GCF of $3x^2$ and $6x$: ☐

$= $ ☐ $($ ☐ $- $ ☐ $)$

⑨ $4x^2 + x$ ← GCF of $4x^2$ and x: ☐

$= $ ☐ $($ ☐ $+ $ ☐ $)$

⑩ $6x^2 - 4x$ ← GCF of $6x^2$ and $4x$: ☐

$= $ ☐ $($ ☐ $- $ ☐ $)$

Identify the GCF to factor each polynomial.

⑪ $5x + 15$

⑫ $4x - 12$

⑬ $18x^2 + 6$

⑭ $8x^2 + 4x + 2$

⑮ $3x^2y + 6x$

⑯ $xy^2 + 2xy$

Factor the polynomials.

⑰ $x(x + 5) + 2(x + 5)$

⑱ $x(x - 3) - 4(x - 3)$

⑲ $x(y + 1) + 2(y + 1)$

⑳ $a(x + 2) + (x + 2)$

㉑ $x(2y + 1) - 2(2y + 1)$

㉒ $y(2y + 1) - x(2y + 1)$

Factor each polynomial. Show your work.

㉓ $ax + ay + 5x + 5y$

㉔ $ax + by + bx + ay$

㉕ $ax - bx + ay - by$

㉖ $xy - 5y + 2x - 10$

㉗ $xy + 2x + 3y + 6$

㉘ $3x^2 + 6x + 4x + 8$

㉙ $x^2 + y + x + xy$

㉚ $5x^2 + 4y + 2xy + 10x$

Hint

A common factor of a polynomial can be

• a monomial:

e.g. $2x^2y + xy$

$= \boxed{xy}(2x + 1)$

↑

common factor: a monomial
with 2 variables

• a binomial:

e.g. $2(x + 1) - y(x + 1)$

$= \boxed{(x + 1)}(2 - y)$

↑

common factor: a binomial

Hint

Put the terms into groups before factoring.

common   common
factor: a factor: b

↓   ↓

e.g. $\boxed{ax + ay} + \boxed{bx + by}$

$= a(x + y) + b(x + y)$

$= (x + y)(a + b)$

Sometimes you need to rearrange the terms to group the like terms before factoring.

e.g. $ax + by + ay + bx$

$= ax + bx + ay + by$

$= x(a + b) + y(a + b)$

$= (x + y)(a + b)$

Expand the polynomials and simplify them.   Show your work.

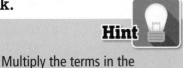

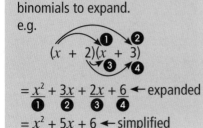

㉛ $(x + 2)(x + 1)$

㉜ $(x + 1)(x - 3)$

Multiply the terms in the
binomials to expand.
e.g.

$(x + 2)(x + 3)$

$= \underline{x^2} + \underline{3x} + \underline{2x} + \underline{6}$ ← expanded

$= x^2 + 5x + 6$ ← simplified

㉝ $(x - 4)(x + 2)$

㉞ $(x + 5)(x + 2)$

㉟ $(x - 1)(x - 8)$

㊱ $(x - 5)(x + 5)$

㊲ $(x - 1)(2x + 3)$

㊳ $(2x + 1)(x + 1)$

㊴ $(x + 6)(3x + 2)$

㊵ $(x - 6)(2x - 1)$

㊶ $(2x + 1)(2x - 1)$

㊷ $(x + y)(x + 2y)$

㊸ $(x^2 - y)(x + y)$

Check whether the factoring or expanding was done correctly.   If not, write the correct answer.

㊹ $4x(2x + 1) = \underline{8x^2 + 4x}$

㊺ $6x^2 + 15x + 3 = \underline{3x(2x + 5 + 1)}$

㊻ $3xy(2x + 6y - 2) = \underline{6x^2y + 18xy - 6xy}$

㊼ $2x - xy - y + 2 = \underline{(x - 1)(y + 2)}$

㊽ $(y - x)(2x + 5) = \underline{-2x^2 - 5x^2 + 2xy + 5y}$

㊾ $(x^2 - 2y)(x + y) = \underline{x^3 + x^2y - 2y^2}$

Answer the questions.

(50) Determine the greatest common factor of the terms in each polynomial.

a. $x^2 + 5x$ b. $2x^2 - 4x + 6$ c. $3y - 2y^2 + y$

d. $8m^2n + 12mn^2$ e. $-6x - 2x + 3$ f. $2a^2b^2 - ab^2 + 5a^2b$

(51) Find the missing factors.

a. $2x^2 + x = (\quad)(2x + 1)$ b. $9y^3 + 12xy - 6y^2 = (\quad)(3y^2 + 4x - 2y)$

c. $10x^2 - 20x + 5xy = (\quad)(2x - 4 + y)$ d. $8x^2 - 4x + 16 = (\quad)(4x^2 - 2x + 8)$

e. $12x^2 - 6x = 3x(\quad)$ f. $5a^2b - ab^2 + 3ab = ab(\quad)$

g. $10xy - 2y^2 + 4y = 2y(\quad)$ h. $-6m^2n + 2mn^2 - 8mn = -2mn(\quad)$

(52) Fully factor each polynomial.

a. $x^3 + 5x^2 - x$ b. $4x^2 + xy + 6x$ c. $12(y + 3) - x(y + 3)$

d. $10(x - 5) + x^2(x - 5)$ e. $2x^3 - 4x^2 - 2x$ f. $x^2y - 2xy^2 + 3xy$

(53) Determine whether each polynomial can be factored further. If so, fully factor it.

a. $5(x - 3y)$ b. $(x + 5)(2x - 4)$ c. $(3x - 1)(2x + 3)$

d. $x(xy + x)(y + 1)$ e. $(2x - 6)(x^2 - 3x)$ f. $(x^2 - 5)(10x + 1)$

(54) Expand the polynomials.

a. $(x + 3)(x - 4)$ b. $(x - 5)(x + 2)$ c. $(2x + 3)(x + 5)$

d. $(x - 8)(2x - 1)$ e. $(x + y)(y + 1)$ f. $(x + 2)(x^2 + y)$

(55) Describe how factoring and expanding a polynomial are related.

(56) Jenny says, "Expanding a polynomial will always result in three terms or more." Is she correct? Give an example to demonstrate.

(57) Write a fully factored expression to represent the perimeter of the rectangle.

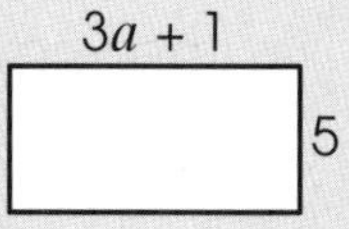

(58) Show that the difference of the squares of two consecutive integers is an odd number.

(59) The product of two integers is divisible by 2. If one of the integers can be represented by $4a + 1$, where a is a whole number, is the other integer an odd or even number? Explain.

(60) A cube is cut along one of its diagonals to form two right triangular prisms. Write a factored polynomial expression to represent the surface area of one right triangular prism.

Chapter 1

1.2 Factorization

Key Ideas

Recall that a trinomial is a polynomial with three terms. Factorization of a trinomial involves expressing it as a product of binomials (polynomials with two terms). However, not all trinomials can be factored. You will learn to identify these trinomials in this chapter.

It is important to understand that factoring is the opposite of expanding, which is about multiplying. Having a good grasp of their relationship will help you understand how to factor polynomials.

Examples

$(x + 1)(x + 2)$ ← factored form
$= x^2 + 2x + x + 2$
$= x^2 + 3x + 2$ ← expanded form

factoring

$x^2 + 3x + 2 = (x + 1)(x + 2)$

expanding

Try these!

Complete the table. Then circle the correct answers.

①

Factors of a Trinomial		Product as a Trinomial	Sum of Constants of the Factors	Product of Constants of the Factors
$(x + 3)$	$(x + 2)$	$x^2 + \quad x + $	$3 + 2 = $	$3 \times 2 = $
$(x - 5)$	$(x - 1)$			
$(x + 4)$	$(x - 5)$			
$(x - 3)$	$(x + 6)$			

② When expanding the product of two binomials,

    a. the sum of the constants becomes the **coefficient of the x term** / **constant** in the trinomial.

    b. the product of the constants becomes the **coefficient of the x term** / **constant** in the trinomial.

③ If both constants in the factors are positive, then the trinomial has a **positive** / **negative** coefficient of x and a **positive** / **negative** constant.

④ If both constants in the factors are negative, then the trinomial has a **positive** / **negative** coefficient of x and a **positive** / **negative** constant.

⑤ If the factors contain one positive and one negative constant, then the constant in the trinomial is always **positive** / **negative** .

Fill in the blanks. Then factor the trinomials.

⑥ $x^2 + 2x + 1$

= $(x + \boxed{})(x + \boxed{})$

sum = 2
product = 1

⑦ $x^2 + 9x + 8$

= $(x + \boxed{})(x + \boxed{})$

sum = 9
product = 8

⑧ $x^2 + 7x + 10$

= $(x + \boxed{})(x + \boxed{})$

sum = 7
product = 10

⑨ $x^2 + 3x + 2$

= $(x + \boxed{})(x + \boxed{})$

sum = 3
product = 2

⑩ $x^2 + 8x + 15$

= $(x + \boxed{})(x + \boxed{})$

sum = 8
product = 15

⑪ $x^2 + 12x + 11$

= $(x + \boxed{})(x + \boxed{})$

sum = 12
product = 11

Hint

A trinomial of the form $x^2 + bx + c$ may be factored into the form $(x + r)(x + s)$, where $b = r + s$, $c = rs$, and r and s are integers.

e.g. $x^2 + 10x + 21$ ← $b = 10$, $c = 21$

= $(x + 3)(x + 7)$ ← $r = 3$, $s = 7$

sum = 10
product = 21

Factor the trinomials.

⑫ $x^2 + 4x + 3$

⑬ $x^2 + 8x + 7$

⑭ $x^2 - 7x + 10$

⑮ $x^2 - 4x + 3$

⑯ $x^2 - 4x - 45$

⑰ $x^2 + 4x - 5$

⑱ $x^2 + 5x - 14$

⑲ $x^2 - 10x + 24$

⑳ $x^2 - 6x + 8$

㉑ $x^2 - 4x - 21$

㉒ $x^2 + 3x - 10$

㉓ $x^2 - 7x - 8$

㉔ $x^2 + 10x + 16$

Hint
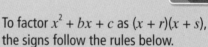

To factor $x^2 + bx + c$ as $(x + r)(x + s)$, the signs follow the rules below.

Trinomial		Factors
b	c	$(r > 0, s > 0)$
+	+	$(x + r)(x + s)$
−	+	$(x - r)(x - s)$
−	−	$(x - r)(x + s)$, where $r > s$
+	−	$(x + r)(x - s)$, where $r > s$

e.g. $x^2 + 2x - 15$ ← $b > 0$, $c < 0$

= $(x + 5)(x - 3)$ ← $r > s$

Determine whether each trinomial can be factored. If yes, factor the trinomial.

㉕ $x^2 + 2x + 2$

㉖ $x^2 + 3x + 6$

㉗ $x^2 + 3x - 4$

㉘ $x^2 - 7x + 10$

㉙ $x^2 + 5x - 6$

㉚ $x^2 - 4x + 8$

㉛ $x^2 + 5x + 9$

㉜ $x^2 - 8x - 9$

Hint

Not all trinomials can be factored. If there are no integers that satisfy $b = r + s$ and $c = rs$, then the trinomial $x^2 + bx + c$ cannot be factored.

e.g. $x^2 + 5x + 1$ ← $b = 5, c = 1$

$1 = 1 \times 1$ or $1 = (-1) \times (-1)$

sum = 2   sum = -2

No pairs of integers that have a product of 1 can have a sum of 5.

So, $x^2 + 5x + 1$ cannot be factored.

Divide out the greatest common factor first. Then fully factor the trinomial. Show your work.

㉝ $3x^2 + 9x + 6$

$= 3(\underline{\quad} + \underline{\quad} + \underline{\quad})$

$= 3(x + \underline{\quad})(x + \underline{\quad})$

㉞ $2x^2 - 4x - 6$

㉟ $4x^2 + 20x + 28$

㊱ $4x^2 - 20x + 24$

㊲ $2x^2 + 2x + 4$

㊳ $6x^2 + 3x + 9$

㊴ $2x^2 + 4x - 6$

㊵ $2x^2 - 4x - 6$

㊶ $6x^2 + 4x + 16$

㊷ $x^3 - 4x^2 - 5x$

㊸ $x^2y - xy - 20y$

㊹ $2x^3 + 10x^2 - 12x$

Fill in the blanks to factor the trinomials.

④⑤ $3x^2 + 5x + 2 \leftarrow a = 3, b = 5, c = 2$

$= 3x^2 + \boxed{}\, x + \boxed{}\, x + 2 \leftarrow$ missing integers: sum = 5, product = 6

↑ b ↑ $a \times c$

④⑥ $6x^2 + 13x + 6 \leftarrow a = 6, b = 13, c = 6$

$= 6x^2 + \boxed{}\, x + \boxed{}\, x + 6 \leftarrow$ missing integers: sum = 13, product = 36

④⑦ $2x^2 + 9x + 4 \leftarrow a = 2, b = 9, c = 4$

$= 2x^2 + \boxed{}\, x + \boxed{}\, x + 4 \leftarrow$ missing integers: sum = 9, product = 8

Hint

To factor trinomials in the form $ax^2 + bx + c$ (where $a \neq 1$) by decomposition, follow the steps below.

❶ Identify the values of a, b, and c.

❷ Find two integers that have a sum of b and a product of a and c.

❸ Replace the term bx with two x terms that have the integers from ❷ as the terms' coefficients.

❹ Factor the polynomials.

e.g. $2x^2 + 7x + 3 \leftarrow a = 2, b = 7, c = 3$

integers: 1, 6

$= 2x^2 + x + 6x + 3 \leftarrow 1 + 6 = 7\ (b)$

                      $1 \times 6 = 6\ (a \times c)$

$= x(2x + 1) + 3(2x + 1)$

$= (2x + 1)(x + 3)$

Factor the trinomials. Show your work.

④⑧ $6x^2 + 7x + 2$

④⑨ $4x^2 + 11x - 3$

⑤⓪ $10x^2 - 19x + 6$

⑤① $8x^2 - 2x - 1$

⑤② $2x^2 + 7x - 4$

⑤③ $3x^2 - 7x + 2$

⑤④ $3x^2 - 8x + 5$

⑤⑤ $4x^2 - 5x + 1$

⑤⑥ $2x^2 - 9x + 4$

Factor the polynomials systematically. Use the boxes to help you.

57. $6x^2 + 7x + 2$

$$= (\underline{}x + \underline{})(\underline{}x + \underline{})$$
$$\quad\quad\;\; p \quad\;\; r \quad\quad\; q \quad\;\; s$$

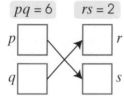

make a combination of →
p, q, r, s so that this is true

58. $2x^2 + x - 3$

$$= (\underline{})(\underline{})$$

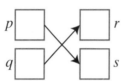

59. $8x^2 - 2x - 1$

$$= (\underline{})(\underline{})$$

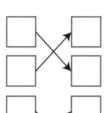

60. $3x^2 + 5x + 2$

61. $2x^2 - 7x + 6$

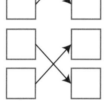

Determine whether each polynomial is factorable. If it is, factor it using the method you prefer.

62. $2x^2 + 9x + 9$

63. $3x^2 + 7x + 4$

64. $3x^2 + 4x + 3$

65. $2x^2 - 7x + 5$

66. $4x^2 - x - 5$

67. $2x^2 - 5x - 9$

68. $5x^2 - 12x + 4$

Answer the questions.

⑥⑨ Factor each trinomial.

a. $x^2 + x - 2$

b. $x^2 + 2x - 3$

c. $x^2 - x - 2$

d. $x^2 + 3x - 4$

e. $x^2 + 7x + 10$

f. $2x^2 - 16x + 30$

g. $3x^2 - 6x - 9$

h. $2x^2 - 4x - 30$

i. $3x^2 - 18x + 24$

⑦⓪ Determine whether each trinomial can be factored.

a. $x^2 + 6x - 10$

b. $x^2 - x - 12$

c. $x^2 - 5x + 8$

d. $x^2 + 4x - 45$

e. $x^2 - 15x + 56$

f. $x^2 - 12x - 24$

⑦① Factor each trinomial.

a. $5x^2 - 7x + 2$

b. $3x^2 - 21x + 18$

c. $2x^2 + 19x + 24$

d. $6x^2 + x - 2$

e. $8x^2 + 10x - 12$

f. $2x^2 + 4x - 70$

g. $4x^3 + 24x^2 + 20x$

h. $10x^2 + 26x - 12$

i. $18x^2 - 15x - 12$

⑦② Determine whether each trinomial can be factored.

a. $5x^2 - 8x + 4$

b. $12x^2 + 5x - 2$

c. $2x^2 - 10x - 48$

d. $3x^2 + 10x - 15$

e. $6x^2 + 18x + 12$

f. $4x^2 - 7x + 16$

⑦③ Find the missing factors.

a. $x^2 - 7x - 18 = (x + 2)\ \boxed{}$

b. $x^2 + 5x - 6 = \boxed{}\ (x - 1)$

c. $2x^2 + 18x^2 + 40 = 2\ \boxed{}\ (x + 5)$

d. $3x^2 + 17x - 6 = (x + 6)\ \boxed{}$

e. $2x^2 - x - 15 = (2x + 5)\ \boxed{}$

f. $6x^2 + 9x - 42 = \boxed{}\ (2x + 7)$

⑦④ Julie says, "Only trinomials may be factored as a product of two binomials." Is she correct? Use an example in your explanation.

⑦⑤ Describe the steps to determine whether a trinomial in the form $ax^2 + bx + c$ can be factored systemically.

⑦⑥ Identify the values of k where $0 < k \le 10$, such that each trinomial can be factored.

a. $x^2 + kx + 8$

b. $2x^2 + kx + 3$

c. $x^2 - 3x - k$

⑦⑦ Determine whether $(x + 2)$ is a factor for each trinomial.

a. $4x^2 + 5x - 6$

b. $3x^2 + 10x - 8$

c. $4x^2 - 2x - 20$

⑦⑧ Factor each trinomial, if possible.

a. $2a^2 + 3ab - b^2$

b. $4m^2 + mn - 3n^2$

c. $2(x + y)^2 + 6(x + y)$

Chapter 1

Key Ideas

Perfect-square trinomials and differences of squares are both special polynomials. They have the factored forms as shown below.

Perfect-square Trinomials

any trinomial that can be factored as the square of a binomial is a perfect-square trinomial

$$a^2 + 2ab + b^2 = (a + b)^2$$
$$a^2 - 2ab + b^2 = (a - b)^2$$

Difference of Squares

any polynomial that contains a subtraction of two squares is a difference of squares:

$$a^2 - b^2 = (a + b)(a - b)$$

Examples

Factor the perfect-square trinomials.

$$a^2 + 2ab + b^2$$
$$x^2 + 10x + 25$$

Think:
$a^2 = x^2 \Rightarrow a = x$
$b^2 = 25 \Rightarrow b = 5$

$$= (x + 5)^2$$
$$\ a\ \ b$$

$$a^2 - 2ab + b^2$$
$$x^2 - 6x + 9$$

Think:
$a^2 = x^2 \Rightarrow a = x$
$b^2 = 9 \Rightarrow b = 3$

$$= (x - 3)^2$$
$$\ a\ \ b$$

Factor the difference of squares.

$$a^2 - b^2$$
$$x^2 - 9$$

Think:
$a^2 = x^2 \Rightarrow a = x$
$b^2 = 9 \Rightarrow b = 3$

$$= (x + 3)(x - 3)$$
$$\ a\ \ b\ \ a\ \ b$$

Try these!

Identify the values of a and b in the polynomials to factor them.

① **Perfect-square Trinomials**

a. $x^2 + 6x + 9$ $a^2 = x^2 \Rightarrow a = \boxed{}$

$= (\boxed{} + \boxed{})^2$ $b^2 = 9 \Rightarrow b = \boxed{}$

b. $x^2 - 8x + 16$ $a^2 = x^2 \Rightarrow a = \boxed{}$

$= (\boxed{} - \boxed{})^2$ $b^2 = 16 \Rightarrow b = \boxed{}$

c. $x^2 + 18x + 81$ $a^2 = \boxed{} \Rightarrow a = \boxed{}$

$= (\boxed{} + \boxed{})^2$ $b^2 = \boxed{} \Rightarrow b = \boxed{}$

d. $x^2 - 10x + 25$ $a^2 = \boxed{} \Rightarrow a = \boxed{}$

$= (\boxed{} - \boxed{})^2$ $b^2 = \boxed{} \Rightarrow b = \boxed{}$

② **Differences of Squares**

a. $x^2 - 4$ $a^2 = x^2 \Rightarrow a = \boxed{}$

$= (\boxed{} + \boxed{})(\boxed{} - \boxed{})$ $b^2 = 4 \Rightarrow b = \boxed{}$

b. $x^2 - 25$ $a^2 = x^2 \Rightarrow a = \boxed{}$

$= (\boxed{} + \boxed{})(\boxed{} - \boxed{})$ $b^2 = 25 \Rightarrow b = \boxed{}$

c. $x^2 - 100$ $a^2 = \boxed{} \Rightarrow a = \boxed{}$

$= (\boxed{} + \boxed{})(\boxed{} - \boxed{})$ $b^2 = \boxed{} \Rightarrow b = \boxed{}$

d. $x^2 - 16$ $a^2 = \boxed{} \Rightarrow a = \boxed{}$

$= (\boxed{} + \boxed{})(\boxed{} - \boxed{})$ $b^2 = \boxed{} \Rightarrow b = \boxed{}$

Factor the perfect-square trinomials.

③ $x^2 + 12x + 36$

④ $x^2 + 10x + 25$

Hint

Don't forget to take the square root of the coefficient of x^2.

e.g. $a^2 = 4x^2$ $b^2 = 9$
     $a = 2x$ $b = 3$

$4x^2 + 12x + 9$
$= (2x + 3)^2$
     a b

⑤ $x^2 - 16x + 64$

⑥ $x^2 - 2x + 1$

⑦ $9x^2 + 6x + 1$

⑧ $4x^2 + 12x + 9$

⑨ $4x^2 - 4x + 1$

⑩ $9x^2 + 12x + 4$

⑪ $25x^2 - 10x + 1$

⑫ $9x^2 - 6x + 1$

⑬ $16x^2 + 8x + 1$

⑭ $25x^2 + 20x + 4$

Factor the polynomial if it is a perfect-square trinomial.

⑮ $x^2 + 18x + 81$

⑯ $x^2 - 12x + 36$

Hint

To determine whether a polynomial is a perfect-square trinomial, follow the steps below.

❶ Find the values of a and b.

❷ Find the value of $2ab$.

❸ Compare $2ab$ with the middle term. If they are the same, then it is a perfect-square trinomial; otherwise, it is not.

e.g. $a = x$ $b = 2$

$x^2 + 3x + 4$

$2ab = 4x$ (not $3x$)

So, this is not a perfect-square trinomial.

⑰ $4x^2 + 20x + 25$

⑱ $9x^2 - 12x + 4$

⑲ $16x^2 + 40x + 100$

⑳ $25x^2 - 90x + 81$

㉑ $25x^2 - 20x + 4$

㉒ $9x^2 - 3x - 2$

Factor the differences of squares.

㉓ $x^2 - 1$

㉔ $x^2 - 144$

㉕ $x^2 - 121$

㉖ $x^2 - 36$

㉗ $25x^2 - 16$

㉘ $4x^2 - 9$

㉙ $4x^2 - 25$

㉚ $9x^2 - 36$

㉛ $64x^2 - 100$

Hint

Remember to take the square root of the coefficient of the x^2 term to determine the value of a.

e.g. $a^2 = 4x^2$ $b^2 = 1$
$a = 2x$ $b = 1$

$4x^2 - 1$
$= (2x + 1)(2x - 1)$
a b a b

Fully factor each polynomial. Show your work.

㉜ $20x^2 - 80$

㉝ $3x^2 - 30x + 75$

Hint

It usually makes our work easier if we factor out the GCF to simplify a polynomial before further factoring.

㉞ $-2x^2 + 28x - 98$

㉟ $4x^2 - 100$

㊱ $4x^2 - 48x + 144$

Answer the questions.

㊲ Todd built a big square using the tiles below. Find a polynomial expression algebraically to represent the area and find the side length of the big square.

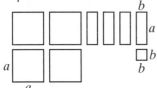

㊳ Write a polynomial expression to represent the shaded area. Fully factor the expression.

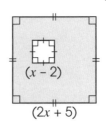

$(x - 2)$

$(2x + 5)$

16   Quadratic Relations (**Grade 10**)

Answer the questions.

㊳ Determine whether each trinomial is a perfect-square trinomial. Factor it if it is.

a. $x^2 + 4x + 4$ b. $x^2 + 8x + 16$ c. $25x^2 + 10x + 1$

d. $x^2 - 10x + 25$ e. $9x^2 - 6x + 4$ f. $4x^2 - 12x + 36$

g. $4x^2 - 20x + 25$ h. $10x^2 - 12x + 25$ i. $9x^2 - 30x + 25$

㊵ Determine whether each is a difference of squares. Factor it if it is.

a. $x^2 + 25$ b. $x^2 - 36$ c. $25x^2 - 50$

d. $4x^2 - 49$ e. $16x^2 - 24$ f. $4x^2 - 30$

g. $25x^2 - 1$ h. $4x^2 - y^2$ i. $9x^2 - 16y^2$

㊶ Factor the polynomials by decomposition. Show the steps.

a. $x^2 - 6x + 9$ b. $x^2 - 49$

c. $4x^2 + 4x + 1$ d. $9x^2 - 4$

Hint

Refer to p. 11 to review how to factor by decomposition.

㊷ Factor.

a. $4x^2 - 40x + 100$ b. $25x^2 - 100$ c. $81x^2 - 25$

d. $9x^2 - 42x + 49$ e. $64x^4 - 144$ f. $18x^4 - 60x^2 + 50$

㊸ Find the missing factors.

a. $4a^2 - 40a + 100 = \boxed{}(a - 5)$ b. $2m^3 - 2mn^2 = (m - n)\boxed{}$

c. $18x^4 - 50y^2 = 2(3x^2 - 5y)\boxed{}$ d. $32a^2 + 16ab + 2b^2 = \boxed{}(4a + b)$

㊹ Determine the term(s) that can be added to turn each into a perfect-square trinomial.

a. $x^2 + 4x$ b. $4x^2 + 1$ c. $16x^2 + 36$

㊺ Determine the smallest positive integer that needs to be added to turn each into a difference of squares.

a. $x^2 - 10$ b. $9x^2 - 39$ c. $16x^2 - 2$

㊻ Show how you can apply the properties of the difference of squares to quickly calculate $29^2 - 19^2$.

㊼ Michael says, "$25 + 4x^2 + 20x$ is a perfect-square trinomial, so when I multiply it by 3, the resulting $60x + 75 + 12x^2$ is still a perfect-square trinomial." Is he correct? Explain.

㊽ A square area is partially covered by square tiles of two different sizes as shown. Consider a and b to be the side lengths of the large and small tiles respectively. Write a polynomial expression to represent the following.

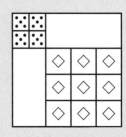

a. the remaining area not covered by tiles

b. the perimeter of the entire square area

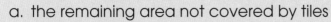

Chapter 1

1.4 Completing the Square

Key Ideas

Completing the square is about factoring part of a polynomial. This technique is useful in expressing quadratic relations in vertex form (which you will learn in Chapter 2). To complete the square, you need to know how to create a perfect-square trinomial.

To create a perfect-square trinomial:

❶ Consider only the terms containing the variable in the expression.

❷ Add a constant that will make the expression a perfect-square trinomial. The constant is half of the coefficient of the x term squared.

$$x^2 + bx + c \leftarrow \text{constant}$$
$$\big(\tfrac{b}{2}\big)^2$$

Examples

Find the constant, c, to make each polynomial a perfect-square trinomial. Then factor it.

$x^2 + 2x + c \leftarrow b = 2 \Rightarrow c = \big(\tfrac{b}{2}\big)^2 = \big(\tfrac{2}{2}\big)^2 = 1$
$= x^2 + 2x + 1 \leftarrow$ perfect-square trinomial
$= (x + 1)^2 \leftarrow$ factored

$4x^2 + 40x + c \leftarrow$ factor out the coefficient of the x^2 term
$= 4(x^2 + 10x + \boxed{}) \leftarrow b = 10 \Rightarrow c = \big(\tfrac{b}{2}\big)^2 = \big(\tfrac{10}{2}\big)^2 = 25$
$= 4(x^2 + 10x + 25) \leftarrow$ perfect-square trinomial
$= 4(x + 5)^2 \leftarrow$ factored

Try these!

Fill in the blanks to make each polynomial a perfect-square trinomial. Then factor it.

① $x^2 + 10x + c$

$= x^2 + 10x + \boxed{} \leftarrow \big(\tfrac{b}{2}\big)^2 = \big(\tfrac{\boxed{}}{2}\big)^2 = \boxed{}$

$= (x + \boxed{})^2$

② $x^2 - 8x + c$

$= x^2 - 8x + \boxed{} \leftarrow \big(\tfrac{b}{2}\big)^2 = \big(\tfrac{\boxed{}}{2}\big)^2 = \boxed{}$

$= (x - \boxed{})^2$

③ $2x^2 + 4x + c$

$= 2(x^2 + 2x + \boxed{}) \leftarrow \big(\tfrac{b}{2}\big)^2 = \big(\tfrac{\boxed{}}{2}\big)^2 = \boxed{}$

$= 2(x + \boxed{})^2$

④ $3x^2 + 24x + c$

$= 3(x^2 + 8x + \boxed{}) \leftarrow \big(\tfrac{b}{2}\big)^2 = \big(\tfrac{\boxed{}}{2}\big)^2 = \boxed{}$

$= 3(x + \boxed{})^2$

⑤ $x^2 + 4x + c$

$= x^2 + 4x + \boxed{}$

$= (x + \boxed{})^2$

⑥ $x^2 + 14x + c$

$= x^2 + 14x + \boxed{}$

$= (x + \boxed{})^2$

⑦ $x^2 - 6x + c$

$= x^2 - \boxed{} + \boxed{}$

$= (\boxed{} - \boxed{})^2$

⑧ $2x^2 - 20x + c$

$= 2(x^2 - 10x + \boxed{})$

$= 2(x - \boxed{})^2$

⑨ $4x^2 + 24x + c$

$= \boxed{}(x^2 + 6x + \boxed{})$

$= \boxed{}(x + \boxed{})^2$

⑩ $5x^2 - 10x + c$

$= \boxed{}(x^2 - \boxed{} + \boxed{})$

$= \boxed{}(x - \boxed{})^2$

Fill in the blanks to make each expression a perfect-square trinomial. Then factor it.

⑪ $x^2 - 2x +$ ____

  $= (x -$ ____$)^2$

⑫ $x^2 - 4x +$ ____

  $=$ _____

⑬ $x^2 - 10x +$ ____

  $=$ _____

⑭ $x^2 + 6x +$ ____

  $=$ _____

⑮ $x^2 - 5x +$ ____

  $=$ _____

⑯ $x^2 + x +$ ____

  $=$ _____

⑰ $2x^2 - 4x + ?$

  ↓

  $2($_____$)$

  $=$ _____

⑱ $2x^2 + 6x + ?$

  ↓

  $2(x^2 + 3x +$ ____$)$

  $= 2(x +$ ____$)^2$

Hint

If the coefficient of the x^2 term is not 1, factor it out from the expression before determining the constant.

Complete the square. Show your work.

Hint

⑲ $x^2 + 6x + 1$

  $= (x^2 + 6x) + 1$ ← create perfect-square trinomials of the terms with variables $(x^2 + 6x)$

  $= (x^2 + 6x + \boxed{} - \boxed{}) + 1$ ← determine the constant; adding and subtracting it results in no change to the expression

  $= (x^2 + 6x + \boxed{}) - \boxed{} + 1$

  $= (x + \boxed{})^2 - \boxed{}$ ← factor the trinomial and simplify

To complete the square, follow the steps below.

❶ Determine the constant that will create a perfect-square trinomial.

❷ Add the constant to the expression and subtract it. Doing this will keep the expression unchanged.

❸ Factor the trinomial and simplify.

⑳ $x^2 + 4x + 2$

㉑ $x^2 - 6x - 2$

㉒ $x^2 - 10x + 3$

㉓ $x^2 + 7x + 1$

㉔ $x^2 - 3x - 5$

Complete the square. Show your work.

㉕ $2x^2 + 16x + 1$

$= 2(x^2 + 8x) + 1$ ← factor out the coefficient of the x^2 term

$= 2(x^2 + 8x + \boxed{} - \boxed{}) + 1$ ← determine the constant; add and subtract it

$= 2(x^2 + 8x + \boxed{}) - \boxed{} + 1$

$= 2(x + \boxed{})^2 - \boxed{}$

㉖ $3x^2 + 12x - 2$

㉗ $2x^2 - 4x + 1$

㉘ $4x^2 + 8x + 5$

㉙ $3x^2 + 9x + 4$

㉚ $2x^2 - 6x - 5$

㉛ $3x^2 + 15x - 2$

Expand each polynomial. Then complete the square to express the polynomial. Show your work.

㉜ $(x + 5)(x + 3)$

㉝ $(x + 7)(x - 3)$

㉞ $(x - 6)(x + 4)$

㉟ $(2x + 3)(2x + 5)$

㊱ $(2x - 1)(2x - 5)$

㊲ $(2x - 5)(2x + 3)$

Answer the questions.

㊳ Determine each value of c so the trinomial is a perfect-square trinomial.

a. $x^2 + 12x + c$ b. $x^2 - 4x + c$

c. $x^2 + 20x + c$ d. $x^2 + 26x + c$

e. $4x^2 + 24x + c$ f. $5x^2 - 10x + c$

g. $4x^2 - 20x + c$ h. $9x^2 - 27x + c$

㊴ Complete the square.

a. $x^2 + 10x$ b. $x^2 - 14x$

c. $x^2 - 12x + 5$ d. $x^2 + 6x + 11$

e. $x^2 + x + 3$ f. $x^2 + 3x - 1$

g. $2x^2 - 16x$ h. $2x^2 + 8x$

i. $2x^2 - 24x + 1$ j. $3x^2 + 48x - 12$

k. $3x^2 + 9x$ l. $5x^2 - 25x + 10$

㊵ Expand and then complete the square.

a. $x(x + 2)$ b. $x(x - 8) + 1$

c. $x(2x - 6)$ d. $x(3x + 4) - 8$

e. $x(2x + 3) - 5$ f. $x(2x + 1) - x(x - 1)$

g. $(x + 2)(x - 8)$ h. $(2x - 1)(2x + 5)$

i. $(x - 1)(x - 2)$ j. $(2x - 5)(x - 1)$

㊶ Can completing the square be applied to all polynomials in the form $ax^2 + bx + c$? If not, specify the conditions when it cannot be applied.

㊷ Liam says, "For $4x^2 + 8x + 1$, I completed the square and got $(2x + 2)^2 - 3$." Without evaluating it, explain why the solution is incorrect.

㊸ Simon and Rex both attempted to complete the square for $3x^2 - 12x + 15$. Identify their errors.

Simon's Solution:

$3x^2 - 12x + 15$

$= 3(x^2 - 4x) + 15$

$= 3(x^2 - 4x + 4) + 15$

$= 3(x - 2)^2 + 15$

Rex's Solution:

$3x^2 - 12x + 15$

$= 3(x^2 - 4x) + 15$

$= 3(x^2 - 4x + 4 - 4) + 15$

$= 3(x^2 - 4x + 4) - 4 + 15$

$= 3(x - 2)^2 - 11$

Things I have learned in this chapter:

- factoring polynomials by common factors and grouping
- expanding polynomials
- factoring trinomials into products of binomials
- factoring perfect-square trinomials and differences of squares
- completing the square

My Notes:

_____

_____

_____

_____

_____

_____

_____

_____

_____

_____

Knowledge and Understanding

Circle the correct answers.

① Which is the greatest common factor in $3x^3 - 12x^2 + 4x$?

    A. 3   B. x

    C. $3x$ D. $4x$

② What is missing in $2x^2 + 6x + 4 = \boxed{}(x + 1)$?

    A. 2   B. $(x + 2)$

    C. $(x - 2)$ D. $2(x + 2)$

③ What is a common factor for all polynomials?

    A. 1   B. 0

    C. x D. none of the above

④ Which is equivalent to $(a - b)(a + 1)$?

    A. $a^2 - b^2$ B. $a^2 - ab - b$

    C. $a^2 - ab + a - b$ D. $a^2 - 2ab + b^2$

⑤ When factoring $x^2 + bx + c$ into $(x + r)(x + s)$, what is the value of c?

    A. $r + s$ B. $r - s$

    C. $s - r$ D. rs

⑥ When factoring $ax^2 + bx + c$ into $(px + r)(qx + s)$, what is the value of b?

    A. pq B. rs

    C. $pq + rs$ D. $ps + rq$

⑦ Which is not a perfect-square trinomial?

    A. $x^2 + 10x + 25$ B. $4x^2 + 6x + 9$

    C. $4x^2 - 8x + 4$ D. $9x^2 - 6x + 1$

⑧ What concept does $(a - b)(a + b) = a^2 - b^2$ demonstrate?

    A. perfect-square trinomial   B. completing the square

    C. difference of squares   D. none of the above

Expand. Show your work.

⑨ $x(x + 5)$

⑩ $3x(2x - y)$

⑪ $(5x - 1)(6x + 2)$

⑫ $3(x + 1)^2$

⑬ $(2a - b)^2$

⑭ $(2x - y)(x + 3y)$

Determine whether each polynomial is fully factored. If not, fully factor it.

⑮ $3(x^2 + x)$

⑯ $x(8x - 2)$

⑰ $x(3x + 2)$

⑱ $2x(x + 4)$

⑲ $2y(x^2 + 3x)$

⑳ $x^2(2x^2 - 4x + 2)$

Match the polynomial with the correct factors, where $r > 0$, $s > 0$, and $r > s$.

㉑ $x^2 + bx + c$ • ⠀⠀⠀ • $(x - r)(x - s)$

$x^2 - bx + c$ • ⠀⠀⠀ • $(x + r)(x - s)$

$x^2 + bx - c$ • ⠀⠀⠀ • $(x + r)(x + s)$

$x^2 - bx - c$ • ⠀⠀⠀ • $(x - r)(x + s)$

Determine the value of c to make each polynomial a perfect-square trinomial. Then factor it.

㉒ $x^2 + 2x + c$

㉓ $x^2 - 14x + c$

㉔ $x^2 + 16x + c$

㉕ $4x^2 - 20x + c$

㉖ $4x^2 + 36x + c$

㉗ $9x^2 - 27x + c$

Fully factor each polynomial. If it cannot be factored, complete the square. Show your work.

㉘ $x^2 - 2x - 1$

㉙ $4x^2 - 20x + 25$

㉚ $x^2 - 5x - 15$

㉛ $3xy - 6x + y^2 - 2y$

㉜ $x^2 + 6x + 1$

㉝ $16x^2 - 8xy + y^2$

㉞ $-3x^2 - 30x - 68$

㉟ $32x^2 - 162$

㊱ $4x^2 - 28x + 40$

㊲ $x^2 - 8x - 12$

㊳ $x^2 - 12x + 35$

㊴ $2x^2 + 5x + 12$

Expand and complete the square.

㊵ $(2x + 5)^2$

㊶ $(3x - 2)(3x + 5)$

㊷ $(2x + 2)(7 - x) - 25$

Determine the missing factors.

㊸ $x^2 - 3x - 40 = (x + 5)()$

㊹ $2x^2 + 16x - 18 = 2()(x - 1)$

㊺ $3x^2 + 6x - 9 = (x - 1)()$

㊻ $10x^2 + 13x - 3 = ()(2x + 3)$

Determine whether $(x - 1)$ is a factor for each polynomial.

㊼ $9x^2 - 4x + 1$

㊽ $-6x^2 + 12x - 6$

㊾ $2x^2 - 4x + 6$

Application

Answer the questions. Show your work.

㊿ The area of a rectangle is represented by $12x^2 + 9x - 3$. If the length of the rectangle is $(4x - 1)$, write an expression to represent the width and the perimeter.

51 Determine the height of the trapezoid.

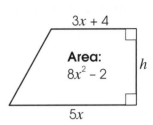

Area:
$8x^2 - 2$

52 Laura has a number of squares and rectangles as shown. How many squares of b^2 does she need to combine all the shapes into one big square?

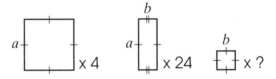

53 James also has squares and rectangles. If he uses only the squares and rectangles he has, what is the largest square he can make, and what pieces are left over?

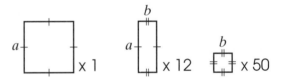

Communication

Answer the questions.

54 Tom says, "The multiples of any perfect-square trinomials are not perfect-square trinomials." Is he correct? Explain using an example.

55 Describe the methodology of determining the value of c of a trinomial in the form $x^2 + bx + c$ to create a perfect-square trinomial.

㊶ Give examples of a trinomial in the form $ax^2 + bx + c$, where when factored, it has 1, 2, or 3 unique factor(s).

㊗ Shaun completed the square of a trinomial and got $(2x + 10)^2 - 1$. Explain why $(2x + 10)^2 - 1$ is not the correct form. Then describe and demonstrate how to convert it into the correct form.

Thinking

Answer the questions. Show your work.

㊙ Show that the sum of the squares of four consecutive integers is an even number.

㊾ Consider $ax^2 - 2ax - 3a$.
   a. Fully factor it.   b. Complete the square.

Chapter 2

Forms of Quadratic Relations

2.1 Parabolas

Key Ideas

The graph of a quadratic relation forms a curved line called a parabola. A parabola is shaped like the letter "U" that opens either upward or downward. It is vertically symmetrical along its axis of symmetry. The intersection of the parabola and the axis of symmetry is the vertex.

Key Features of a Parabola

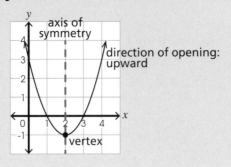

Examples

Identify the key features of the parabolas.

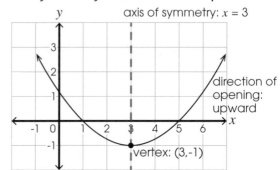

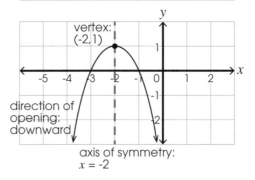

Try these!

Fill in the blanks.

①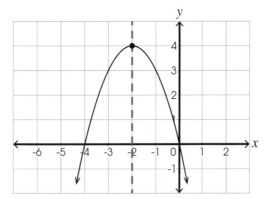

   a.   vertex: (-2,   )

   b.   axis of symmetry: $x =$

   c.   direction of opening:

②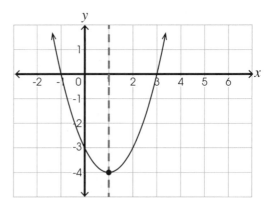

   a.   vertex: (,-4)

   b.   axis of symmetry: $x =$

   c.   direction of opening:

Determine the intercepts of the parabolas. Then answer the questions.

③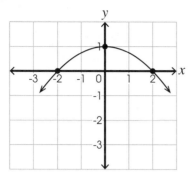

④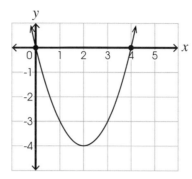

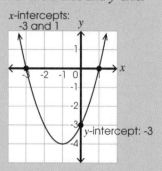
x-intercepts: _____

y-intercept: _____

x-intercepts: _____

y-intercept: _____

⑤ What does it mean for a graph to have no x-intercepts? Describe its parabola.

_____

_____

⑥ What must the y-coordinate of the x-intercept be for a parabola that has one x-intercept?

_____

Find the key features of the parabolas. Complete the table.

⑦

A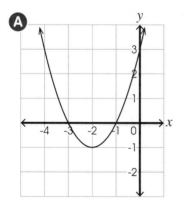

B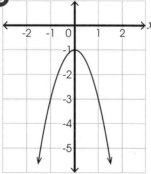

C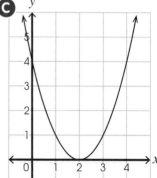

	x-intercept(s)	y-intercept	axis of symmetry	vertex	direction of opening
A					
B					
C					

Write the optimal value of each parabola and check to show whether it is a maximum or minimum value.

⑧

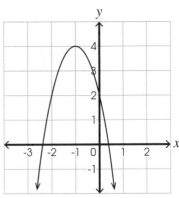

optimal value: _____

○ maximum

○ minimum

⑨

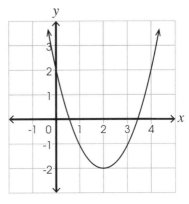

optimal value: _____

○ maximum

○ minimum

Use the given properties to sketch each graph. Then find the remaining properties.

⑩ vertex: (2,4)   zeros: 0 and 4

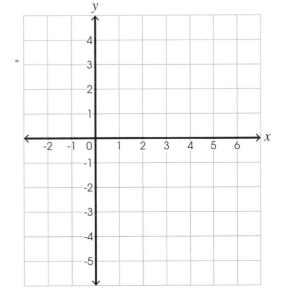

direction of opening: _____

axis of symmetry: _____

optimal value: _____

max. or min.: _____

y-intercept: _____

⑪ y-intercept: 0   vertex: (-2,-4)

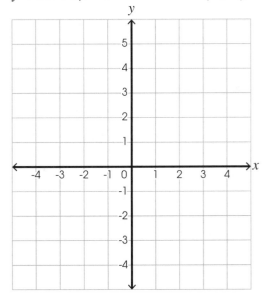

direction of opening: _____

axis of symmetry: _____

optimal value: _____

max. or min.: _____

y-intercept: _____

Complete the table of values. Find the second differences. Then sketch the graphs and answer the questions.

⑫ $y = x^2 - 1$

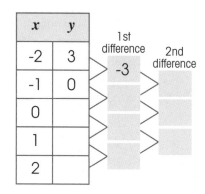

⑬ $y = -x^2 - 2x + 3$

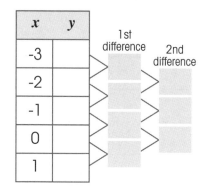

Hint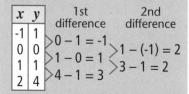

Second differences are found by subtracting consecutive first differences. In a quadratic relation, the second differences are constant and not zero.

e.g. $y = x^2$

x	y	1st difference	2nd difference
-1	1	$0 - 1 = -1$	$1 - (-1) = 2$
0	0	$1 - 0 = 1$	$3 - 1 = 2$
1	1	$4 - 1 = 3$	
2	4		

A positive second difference means the parabola opens upward. A negative second difference means the parabola opens downward.

⑭ Sketch the graphs and label them.

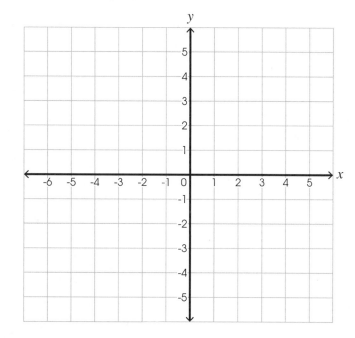

⑮ Circle the correct answers.

a. $y = x^2 - 1$
- 2nd difference: **positive / negative**
- direction of opening: **upward / downward**

b. $y = -x^2 - 2x + 3$
- 2nd difference: **positive / negative**
- direction of opening: **upward / downward**

Write "T" for the true statements and "F" for the false ones.

⑯ The vertex of a parabola that has two zeros is always located halfway between the zeros. _____

⑰ If a parabola opens upward, it must have a maximum. _____

⑱ The y-intercept must always exist in a parabola. _____

⑲ In a quadratic equation, the first differences are constant. _____

⑳ It is possible for a graph to not have any x-intercepts. _____

Determine the direction of opening and *y*-intercept of the parabola of each quadratic relation. Then write the letters in the circles to match.

㉑

Quadratic Relation	Direction of Opening	*y*-intercept
A $y = x^2 - 2x + 1$	_____	_____
B $y = 2x^2 - x - 1$	_____	_____
C $y = -2x^2 + 2x + 1$	_____	_____
D $y = -\dfrac{1}{2}x^2 + x - 1$	_____	_____

Hint

The standard form of a quadratic relation expresses terms in order of descending powers.

Standard Form
$$y = ax^2 + bx + c, \, a \neq 0$$

y-intercept

if $a > 0$, opens upward
if $a < 0$, opens downward

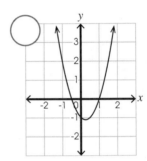
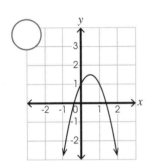
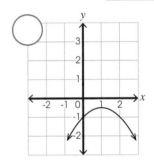
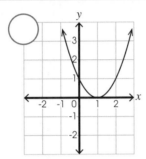

Find the axis of symmetry with the given quadratic relations in standard form. Then answer the question.

Hint

The values of a and b in the standard form can be used to determine the axis of symmetry.

$$x = -\dfrac{b}{2a}$$

e.g. $y = 2x^2 + 4x - 1$

axis of symmetry:
$$x = -\dfrac{4}{2(2)} = -1$$

㉒ $y = x^2 + 2x + 5$

axis of symmetry:

$$x = -\frac{\boxed{}}{2(\,\boxed{}\,)} = \boxed{}$$

㉓ $y = -2x^2 + x - 6$

axis of symmetry:

㉔ $y = \dfrac{1}{2}x^2 + 3x + 2$

axis of symmetry:

㉕ $y = -\dfrac{1}{4}x^2 - 6x + 1$

axis of symmetry:

㉖ The standard form of a quadratic relation is given. Can the coordinates of the vertex be found? Describe your reasoning. If it can be found, find the vertex of $y = 2x^2 + 4x - 1$.

_____

_____

_____

Answer the questions.

㉗ For each graph, identify the axis of symmetry, vertex, zeros, and y-intercept.

a. 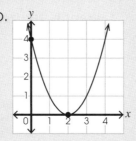 b. 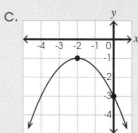 c. 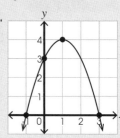 d.

㉘ Find the second differences to determine whether each table of values could represent a quadratic relation. If it could, determine the direction of opening of its parabola.

a.
x	-2	-1	0	1	2
y	-1	2	7	14	23

b.
x	0	1	2	3	4
y	3	6	12	24	48

c.
x	4	2	0	-2	-4
y	0	4	4	0	-8

㉙ Sketch the graphs with the given properties.

a. vertex at (7,2); x-intercepts are 5 and 9

b. zeros at (-3,0) and (3,0); y-intercept is 5

Hint

A parabola is symmetrical.

㉚ A quadratic relation has two zeros. Its second differences are positive.

a. Is the optimal value a maximum or minimum?

b. Is the optimal value a positive or negative number?

㉛ A quadratic relation only has one zero at (6,0). Its second differences are negative.

a. Explain what it means for a graph to have only one x-intercept.

b. What is the vertex of the quadratic relation?

c. Is the optimal value a maximum or minimum? Explain how you know.

㉜ Determine the direction of opening, y-intercept, and axis of symmetry of each quadratic equation in standard form.

a. $y = x^2 + 2x - 1$ b. $y = -x^2 - 4x + 2$

c. $y = 6x - \frac{1}{2}x^2 - 1$ d. $y = 7 + 5x^2$

Hint

Rearrange the terms if needed.

M A T H   I R L

Parabolas are not just present in the study of mathematics; there are also many examples in real life. A stream of water from a fountain often creates an arc that is parabolic in nature, as are many naturally occurring curvatures. Many architectural designs incorporate arches, which also resemble parabolas. Scan this QR code to learn more examples of parabolas.

Chapter 2

2.2 Factored Form

A quadratic relation can be written in the factored form.

Factored Form

$y = a(x - r)(x - s)$

zeros: r and s

In the factored form of a quadratic relation, the zeros can be identified by inspection.

Examples

Identify the zeros of each quadratic relation.

$y = (x - 1)(x - 3)$

zeros: 1 and 3

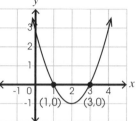

$y = \frac{1}{2}(x - 1)(x + 3)$

$y = \frac{1}{2}(x - 1)(x - -3)$

zeros: 1 and -3

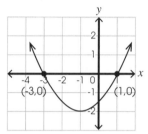

Determine the zeros of each quadratic relation. Then match it with the sketch of its graph. Write the letter.

① **A** $y = (x - 2)(x - 3)$

zeros: 2,

B $y = -\frac{1}{2}(x - 2)(x + 3)$

zeros: 2,

C $y = 2(x - 2)(x + 3)$

zeros: , -3

D $y = -(x + 2)(x - 3)$

zeros: , 3

E $y = \frac{1}{2}(x + 2)(x - 3)$

zeros: ,

F $y = -(x - 2)(x - 3)$

zeros: ,

Try these!

Hint

Similar to the standard form of a quadratic relation, the graph's direction of opening can be determined by the value of a.

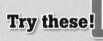

$y = a(x - r)(x - s)$

if $a > 0$, opens upward
if $a < 0$, opens downward

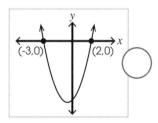

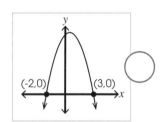

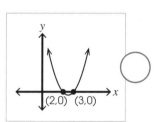

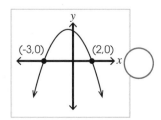

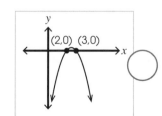

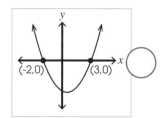

For each graph, find the axis of symmetry.

②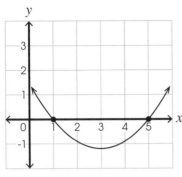

$$x = \frac{\boxed{} + \boxed{}}{2} = \boxed{}$$

③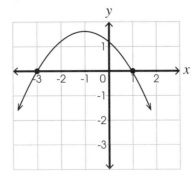

Practice

Hint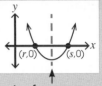

To find the axis of symmetry, find the mean of the zeros.

axis of symmetry:

$$x = \frac{r+s}{2}$$

④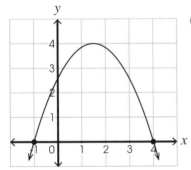

⑤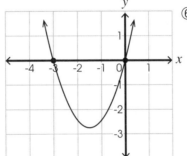

⑥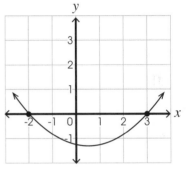

Find the key features of each quadratic relation in factored form.

⑦ $y = 2(x - 4)(x + 6)$

- zeros: ____ , ____

- axis of symmetry: $x =$ ____

- vertex: (____ , ____)

- y-intercept: ____

⑧ $y = \frac{1}{2}(x + 1)(x - 3)$

- zeros: ____ , ____

- axis of symmetry: _____

- vertex: _____

- y-intercept: ____

Hint

To find the vertex, substitute the axis of symmetry into the relation.

To find the y-intercept, determine the value of y when $x = 0$.

e.g. $y = (x - 1)(x + 2)$

Find the y-intercept.
$y = (0 - 1)(0 + 2)$
$y = -2$
↑
y-intercept

⑨ $y = -(x - 2)(x - 6)$

- zeros: _____

- axis of symmetry: _____

- vertex: _____

- y-intercept: ____

⑩ $y = -3(x + 3)(x + 1)$

- zeros: _____

- axis of symmetry: _____

- vertex: _____

- y-intercept: ____

For each quadratic relation in factored form, find the key features and use the information to sketch its graph.

⑪

	$y = (x + 3)(x + 1)$	$y = x(x - 2)$	$y = 2(x - 2)^2$
zero(s)			
vertex			
y-intercept			

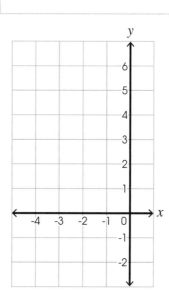
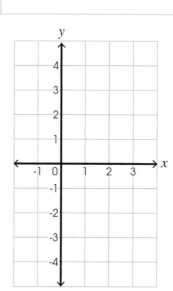
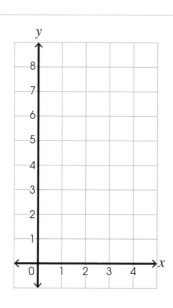

Graph each quadratic relation and label it.

⑫ $y = -x(x + 4)$ ⑬ $y = \dfrac{1}{3}(x + 3)(x - 3)$

   • zeros: _____

   • vertex: _____

   • y-intercept: ____

⑭ $y = \dfrac{1}{2}(x + 5)(x - 1)$ ⑮ $y = -\dfrac{1}{4}(x + 2)(x - 4)$

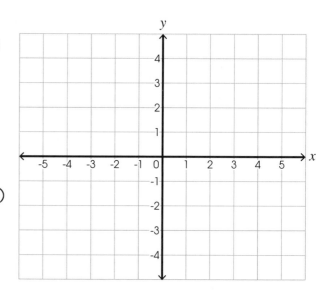

Find the factored form of the quadratic relation of each graph.

⑯

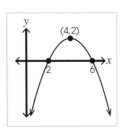

⑰

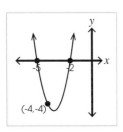

⑱

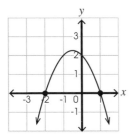

⑲

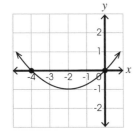

Hint

Follow the steps below to determine the factored form of a quadratic relation.

e.g.

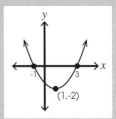

❶ Substitute the zeros into the factored form.

$y = a(x - (-1))(x - 3)$
$y = a(x + 1)(x - 3)$

❷ Substitute any point other than the zeros into the relation to find a.

$-2 = a(1 + 1)(1 - 3)$
$-2 = a(2)(-2)$
$a = \dfrac{1}{2}$

❸ Substitute the value of a into the relation.

$y = \dfrac{1}{2}(x + 1)(x - 3)$

The quadratic relation:
$\dfrac{1}{2}(x + 1)(x - 3)$

Find the factored form of each quadratic relation with the given information.

⑳ • zeros: -1, 5
    • point: (4,10)

㉑ • zeros: -8, 4
    • vertex: (-2,-4)

㉒ • zero: -6
    • y-intercept: 9

Change the factored form of each quadratic relation to the standard form. Show your work. Then find the zeros and the *y*-intercept.

㉓ $y = -(x - 8)(x + 1)$

㉔ $y = 4(x)(x - 3)$

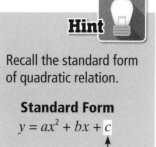

Hint

Recall the standard form of quadratic relation.

Standard Form
$$y = ax^2 + bx + \boxed{c}$$
↑
y-intercept

zeros: _____ ← use factored form

y-intercept: _____ ← use standard form

zeros: _____

y-intercept: _____

㉕ $y = -5(x + 9)^2$

㉖ $y = \dfrac{1}{2}(x + 3)(x + 2)$

㉗ $y = -\dfrac{3}{4}(x - 2)(x + 6)$

zeros: _____

y-intercept: ____

zeros: _____

y-intercept: ____

zeros: _____

y-intercept: ____

Given the following information, find the quadratic relations in standard form.

㉘   zeros: 4, -2
     vertex: (1,-27)

㉙   zeros: 0, 8
     vertex: (4,8)

㉚   zero: 6
     y-intercept: 6

Answer the questions.

㉛ For the following quadratic relations, find the x-intercepts, vertices, and y-intercepts. Then sketch their graphs.

   a. $y = (x - 4)(x + 2)$

   b. $y = \frac{1}{2}(x - 2)(x + 2)$

   c. $y = -2(x - 1)^2$

   d. $y = \frac{3}{2}(x + 3)(x - 1)$

㉜ Change the following quadratic relations from factored form to standard form. Then state their zeros and y-intercepts.

   a. $y = (x + 2)(x - 7)$

   b. $y = -2(x - 3)(x + 9)$

   c. $y = \frac{1}{2}(x - 6)^2$

   d. $y = -x(x - 100)$

㉝ Find the quadratic relation of each parabola in both factored form and standard form.

   a.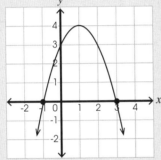
   b.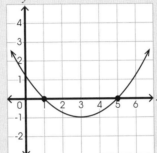
   c.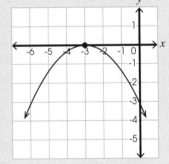

㉞ Find the standard form of the quadratic relations with the given information.

   a. a parabola with zeros at -5 and 1 and has a y-intercept of 15

   b. a parabola with zeros at -3 and -1 and has a vertex at (-2,2)

   c. a parabola with zeros at 0 and -12 and has a minimum of -3

   d. a parabola with zeros at 0 and -6 and has a maximum of 3

Hint

The point that is a minimum or maximum lies on the axis of symmetry.

㉟ Given that the zeros of a parabola are 7 and -3, give three possible quadratic relations in factored form for this parabola.

㊱ An arch of a highway overpass is in the shape of a parabola. The arch spans a distance of 12 m from one side of the road to the other. The highest point of the arch is 4 m.

   a. Sketch the quadratic relation with the vertex of the arch lying on the y-axis and the road on the x-axis.

   b. Find the equation of the arch.

   c. How high is the arch when it is 3 m from each end horizontally?

Chapter 2

2.3 Vertex Form

Key Ideas

You have learned about the standard form and factored form of quadratic relations. In the standard form, the y-intercept and direction of opening can be easily identified, whereas in the factored form, the zeros can be found by inspection.

The vertex form is another common form of quadratic relations.

Vertex Form

$$y = a(x - h)^2 + k$$

vertex: (h,k)

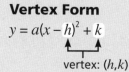

The vertex form allows you to find the vertex easily. It is also commonly used to represent a quadratic relation when performing transformations, which you will learn in Chapter 3.

Examples

Identify the vertex of each quadratic relation.

$$y = (x - 1)^2 + 2$$

vertex: (1,2)

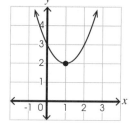

Be mindful of the values of h and k. Make sure that they have the correct signs.

$$y = (x + 1)^2 - 3$$
$$= (x - \text{-}1)^2 + \text{-}3$$

vertex: (-1,-3)

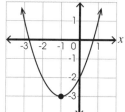

Identify the vertex and find the y-intercept of each quadratic relation. Then write the letters in the circles to match.

Try these!

①

Ⓐ $y = (x - 1)^2 + 1$

  a. vertex:

    (1,   )

  b. y-intercept:

    $y = (0 - \boxed{})^2 + 1$

    $y = \boxed{}$

Ⓑ $y = -2(x - 1)^2 + 1$

  a. vertex:

    (,1)

  b. y-intercept:

    $y = -2(0 - 1)^2 + \boxed{}$

    $y = \boxed{}$

Ⓒ $y = (x + 1)^2 - 1$

  a. vertex:

    (,   )

  b. y-intercept:

    $y = \boxed{}$

    $y = \boxed{}$

Ⓓ $y = -\dfrac{1}{2}(x + 1)^2 - 1$

  a. vertex:

    (,   )

  b. y-intercept:

    $y = \boxed{}$

    $y = \boxed{}$

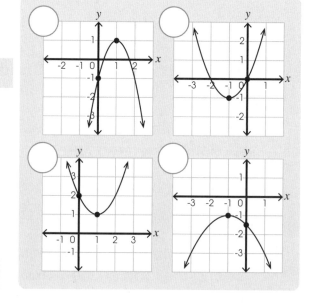

Find the vertex, *y*-intercept, and direction of opening of each quadratic relation. Then label its graph.

② $y = (x - 3)^2 - 5$

a. vertex: _____

b. *y*-intercept: _____

c. direction of opening:

_____

③ $y = -\frac{1}{3}(x + 3)^2$

a. vertex: _____

b. *y*-intercept: _____

c. direction of opening:

_____

④ $y = \frac{1}{2}(x + 2)^2 - 1$

a. vertex: _____

b. *y*-intercept: _____

c. direction of opening:

_____

⑤ $y = -\frac{1}{4}(x - 2)^2$

a. vertex: _____

b. *y*-intercept: _____

c. direction of opening:

_____

Hint

To determine whether a quadratic relation opens upward or downward, identify the value of *a* in its vertex form.

$$y = a(x - h)^2 + k$$

if $a > 0$, opens upward
if $a < 0$, opens downward

e.g. $y = 2(x - 4)^2 - 1$

> 0; upward

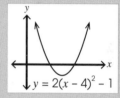
$y = 2(x - 4)^2 - 1$

$y = -2(x - 4)^2 - 1$

< 0; downward

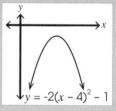
$y = -2(x - 4)^2 - 1$

⑥

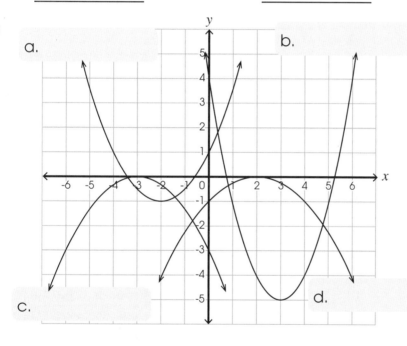

a.

b.

c.

d.

Find the features of the parabola of each quadratic relation written in vertex form.

⑦

quadratic relation	vertex	*y*-intercept	direction of opening	axis of symmetry	optimal value	max. or min.
$y = (x - 2)^2 + 1$						
$y = -(x + 3)^2 - 2$						
$y = -3(x - 5)^2 + 10$						
$y = \frac{1}{4}(x + 6)^2$						

Sketch the graph of each quadratic relation and label it.

⑧ $y = -(x - 3)^2 + 6$
  - vertex: (3,6)
  - y-intercept: -3
  - opens downward

⑨ $y = 2(x + 2)^2 - 3$

⑩ $y = \dfrac{1}{2}(x - 3)^2 - 2$

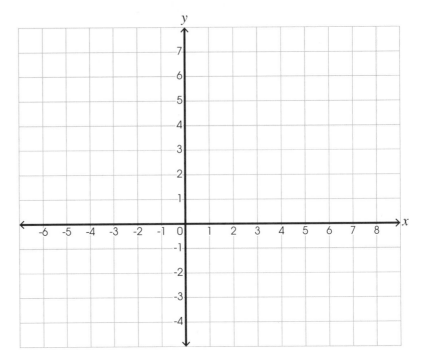

Find the equation with the given properties in vertex form. Show your work.

⑪ vertex: (1,3) ◄— h and k
  point: (2,5) ◄— x and y

$$\overset{\displaystyle y}{\downarrow} \qquad \overset{\displaystyle x}{\downarrow} \quad \overset{\displaystyle h}{\downarrow} \qquad \overset{\displaystyle k}{\downarrow}$$

$$\boxed{} = a(\ \boxed{}\ - \ \boxed{}\ )^2 + \boxed{}$$

$y = $ _____

_____

⑫ vertex: (1,-2)
  point: (5,-10)

⑬ vertex: (1,2)
  y-intercept: -1

_____

⑭ vertex: (-2,9)
  x-intercept: 1

_____

Hint

The equation of a quadratic relation can be found using the vertex and a point that lies on its parabola.

❶ Substitute the vertex (h,k) and the coordinates of another point (x,y) into the vertex form.

❷ Solve for a.

❸ Write the vertex form using the values of a, h, and k.

e.g. vertex: (2,1)
    point: (3,4)

$$\overset{\displaystyle y}{\downarrow} \quad \overset{\displaystyle x}{\downarrow}\ \overset{\displaystyle h}{\downarrow}\quad \overset{\displaystyle k}{\downarrow}$$

$4 = a(3 - 2)^2 + 1$
$4 = a(1)^2 + 1$
$4 = a + 1$
$a = 3$

Equation: $y = 3(x - 2)^2 + 1$
    $\uparrow \qquad \uparrow \quad \uparrow$
    $a \qquad h \quad k$

Find the quadratic relation of the sketch of each graph.

⑮

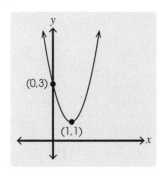

⑯

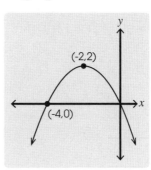

⑰

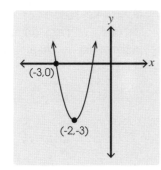

⑱

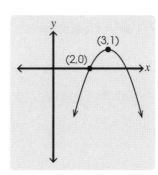

⑲

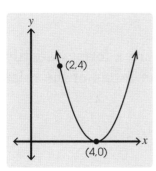

⑳

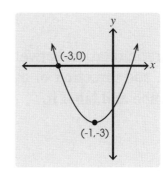

Find the quadratic relations of the graphs.

㉑

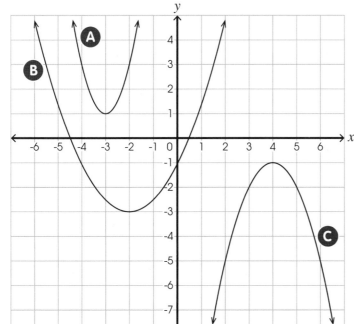

Ⓐ _____

Ⓑ _____

Ⓒ _____

Convert the quadratic relations from vertex form to standard form and vice versa.

㉒

vertex form ⟶ standard form

a. $y = (x + 2)^2 - 5$

$y = (\underline{\hspace{1cm}})(\underline{\hspace{1cm}}) - 5$

$y = \underline{\hspace{3cm}} - 5$

$y = \underline{\hspace{3cm}}$

b. $y = 2(x - 4)^2 + 7$

㉓

standard form ⟶ vertex form

a. $y = x^2 + 2x + 3$

b. $y = 3x^2 + 12x - 9$

> **Hint**
>
> Revisit the concept of factoring and expanding polynomials in Chapter 1.

Convert each quadratic relation between standard form and vertex form. Identify the vertex, y-intercept, and direction of opening by inspecting the forms of the relation. Then sketch the graph and label it.

㉔ $y = (x + 2)^2 - 3$

㉕ $y = -5x^2 + 10x - 4$

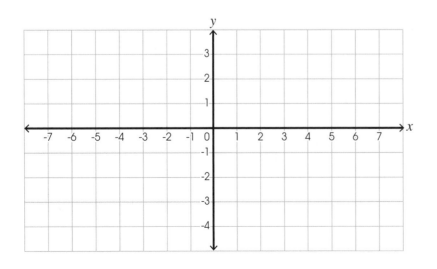

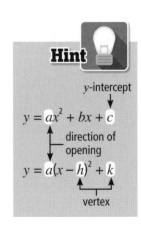

Hint

y-intercept

$y = ax^2 + bx + c$

direction of opening

$y = a(x - h)^2 + k$

vertex

Answer the questions.

㉖ For each quadratic equation, identify the vertex, axis of symmetry, optimal value, whether it is a maximum or minimum, the direction of opening, and the y-intercept.

a. $y = (x + 3)^2 - 5$ b. $y = -(x - 3)^2 + 10$ c. $y = 2(x + 5)^2$

d. $y = -(x - 4)^2 + 1$ e. $y = \frac{1}{2}(x - 2)^2 + 4$ f. $y = -5(x - 4)^2 + 3$

㉗ Convert the vertex form into standard form and vice versa.

a. $y = (x - 4)^2 + 1$ b. $y = -3(x + 3)^2$ c. $y = 2(x - 1)^2 - 5$

d. $y = 2x^2 + 12x + 18$ e. $y = x^2 - 2x - 1$ f. $y = -3x^2 + 12x - 11$

㉘ Write an equation for each parabola in vertex form.

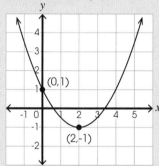 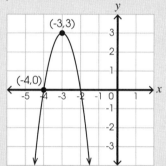 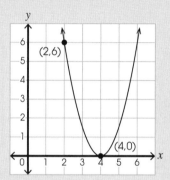

㉙ Write an equation for each quadratic relation in standard form.

a. a parabola with a vertex at (3,-2) that passes through (4,-5)

b. a parabola with a vertex at (-1,7) that has a y-intercept of 5

c. a parabola with zeros at 4 and 10 and has a maximum of 18

d. a parabola with zeros at -4 and 8 and has a minimum of -36

㉚ Describe the advantages of writing a quadratic equation in standard form and in vertex form.

㉛ Explain why in either standard form or vertex form, the value of a cannot be zero for a quadratic relation.

㉜ A dome has a cross section in the shape of a parabolic arch with the equation $y = -\frac{1}{45}x^2 + 20$. Determine which graph shown on the right represents the arch. Explain.

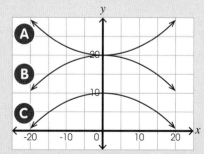

㉝ Consider two parabolas. The first parabola has the equation $y = (x - 3)^2$. The second parabola has a vertex at (-2,5) and passes through the vertex of the first parabola. What is the equation of the second parabola in standard form?

㉞ Consider the parabola with the equation $y = -(x - 3)^2 + 1$. What are its domain (the set of values x may take) and range (the set of values y may take)?

Chapter 2

2.4 Applications

The equations of a quadratic model can represent any real-life scenario that resembles a parabolic curve.

As you have learned, all quadratic relations can be expressed in both standard form and vertex form. If a quadratic equation can also be expressed in factored form, then it has zeros.

When given a set of points, you may use a curve of good fit to model a parabolic curve.

A curve of good fit is a curve that has a good estimation to a set of points.

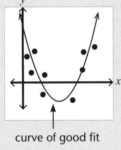

curve of good fit

Examples

Find a curve of good fit for the set of data points and an equation to represent the curve.

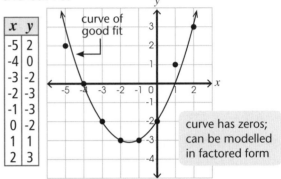

x	y
-5	2
-4	0
-3	-2
-2	-3
-1	-3
0	-2
1	1
2	3

curve has zeros; can be modelled in factored form

$y = a(x + 4)(x - 1)$ ← substitute the zeros in factored form

$-2 = a(0 + 4)(0 - 1)$ ← (0,-2) lies on the curve; substitute

$-2 = a(4)(-1)$ ← find a

$a = \dfrac{1}{2}$

equation: $y = \dfrac{1}{2}(x + 4)(x - 1)$

Make a scatter plot with each set of data. Draw a curve of good fit. Then find the equation of the curve.

Try these!

①
x	y
1	0
1.5	1.5
2	3
2.5	4
3	4
3.5	3.5
4	3
4.5	2
5	0

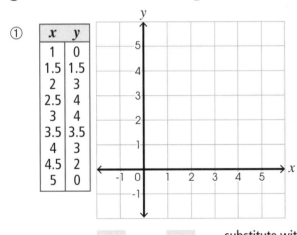

②
x	y
-3	3
-2.5	1.5
-2	0
-1	-1.5
0	-3
1	-3
2	-2.5
3	0
3.5	2

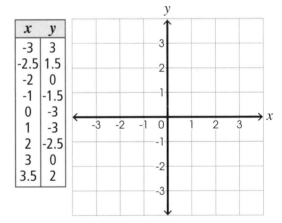

$y = a(x - \boxed{})(x - \boxed{})$ ← substitute with zeros of curve

$\boxed{} = a(\boxed{} - \boxed{})(\boxed{} - \boxed{})$ ← substitute x and y with a point on curve

$a = \boxed{}$ ← value of a

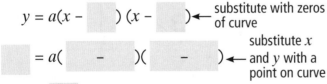

$y = \underline{}$

$y = a(x - \boxed{})(x - \boxed{})$

$\boxed{} = a(\boxed{} + \boxed{})(\boxed{} - \boxed{})$ ←

find a

$a = \boxed{}$

$y = \underline{}$

Read about each scenario. Plot the points and find a curve of good fit. Determine an equation to represent the scenario and answer the questions.

③ A ball was thrown. The horizontal distance it travelled and its height are recorded.

Distance (m)	2	3	4	5	6	7	8	9	10
Height (m)	0	6	12	16	16	15	13	6	1

a. Plot the points and draw a curve of good fit.

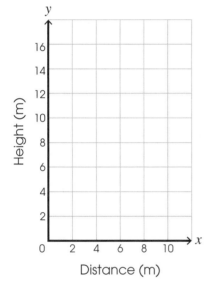

Distance (m)

b. Find the equation in vertex form that represents the curve.

c. Use the equation to estimate the height when the distance travelled was 4.5 m.

④ A swimmer dived into a pool. The horizontal distance travelled and water level are recorded.

Distance (m)	0	1	2	3	4	5	6	7
Water Level (m)	0	-2.5	-5	-6	-6	-4.5	-3	0

a. Plot the points and draw a curve of good fit.

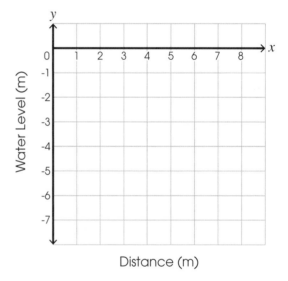

Distance (m)

b. Find the equation in factored form that represents the curve.

c. Use the equation to estimate the distance travelled when the swimmer was 5 m under the water. (Hint: Express the equation in factored form and set each factor to 0.)

Read each scenario and answer the questions.

⑤ The loop of a roller coaster is modelled by a parabolic curve.

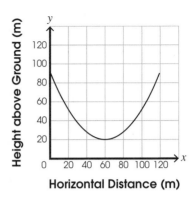

Horizontal Distance (m)

  a. What is its height above ground at its lowest point?

  b. The loop's height is 52 m when its horizontal distance is 100 m. Find the equation in vertex form to model this loop.

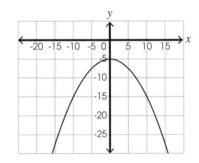

Hint

For a parabola that has no zeros, find the equation in vertex form, given that the vertex is known.

⑥ Jack drew a parabola to resemble part of a stream of water from a drinking water fountain. Write an equation to represent the stream of water.

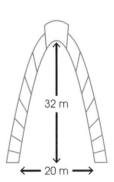

⑦ A structural arch is shown with the measurements.

  a. Write an equation to model the underside of the arch.

  b. What is the width of the arch at 24 m high?

32 m

← 20 m →

Solve the problems. Show your work.

⑧ A school is hosting a concert for fundraising. The profit P, is modelled by $P = -0.8x^2 + 56x - 480$, where x is the cost of a ticket in dollars.

Hint

When modelling problems that involve maximum or minimum values with equations, it is helpful to have the equations written in vertex form.

a. Write the equation for the model in vertex form.

b. What is the maximum profit?

c. What costs of the tickets will result in a profit of $0?

⑨ The average cost of 3-D printing a figurine is modelled by the equation $C = 0.2n^2 - 16n + 330$, where C is the cost per figurine and n is the number of figurines produced.

a. How many figurines should be produced to minimize the average cost?

b. How many figurines produced will lead to an average cost of $30 per figurine?

⑩ A dive off of a diving board is approximated by $h = -5t^2 + 10t + 3$, where h is the height above water in metres and t is the time in seconds after the diver left the board.

a. What was the diver's maximum height above water?

b. How high is the diving board?

Read about each scenario. Write an equation to represent it. Then answer the questions.

⑪ The ticket price of a hockey arena that seats 800 people is $4 per person. A survey shows that for every $2 increase in ticket price, attendance will fall by 100 people.

a. Write a quadratic equation to model the total revenue.

Let R be the revenue and n be the number of $2 increases.

price   no. of tickets sold

$R = (4 + \underline{\quad})(800 - \underline{\quad})$

b. Write the equation in vertex form.

c. Use the vertex form to determine the maximum revenue.

d. What ticket price will maximize revenue?

⑫ A bakery finds that a 25-cent increase in the price of muffins results in 50 fewer muffins sold. The price of $3 per muffin results in the sale of 1000 muffins.

a. Write a quadratic equation to model the total revenue.

b. Write the equation in vertex form.

c. Use the vertex form to determine the greatest revenue.

d. What price of muffins will result in the greatest revenue?

Answer the questions.

⑬ Consider the sets of data.

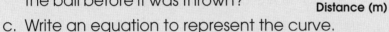

A

x	-4	-3	-2	-1	0	1	2
y	0	-2.5	-4	-4.5	-4	-2.5	0

B

x	-4	-3	-2	-1	0	1	2
y	-5	-1	3	4	3	1	-5

a. Make a scatter plot for each set and find a curve of good fit.

b. Find the equation of each curve in factored form and vertex form.

⑭ The path of a ball is modelled by the curve as shown.

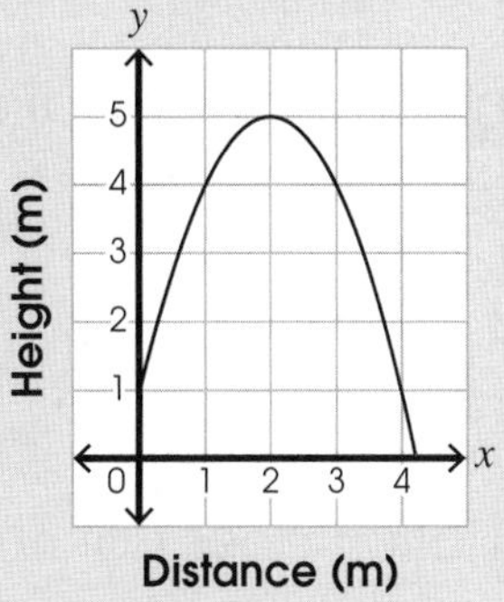

a. What was the maximum height of the ball?

b. What was the initial height of the ball before it was thrown?

c. Write an equation to represent the curve.

(Graph: y-axis labelled "Height (m)" with values 1–5; x-axis labelled "Distance (m)" with values 1, 2, 3, 4; showing a parabola opening downward.)

⑮ A flare was released into the air following the path modelled by $h = -5(t - 6)^2 + 182$, where h is the height in metres and t is the time in seconds.

a. What was the flare's maximum height?

b. What was the flare's initial height?

c. How long was the flare in the air?

⑯ If a toy rocket is launched vertically upward from the ground level, its trajectory is modelled by $h = -16(t - 4)^2 + 256$, where h is the height in metres and t is the time in seconds.

a. How long will it take for the rocket to reach its maximum height?

b. What is its maximum height?

c. How long will it take for the rocket to reach the ground?

⑰ An artisan can sell 120 ornaments per week at $4 per ornament. For every $0.50 decrease in price, 20 more ornaments can be sold. At what price will the revenue be maximized?

⑱ A store sells an average of 60 TVs per month at an average of $800 per unit. For every $20 increase in price, the store sells one fewer unit. What is the price that will maximize revenue?

Things I have learned in this chapter:

• identifying features of a parabola, including the vertex, axis of symmetry, direction of opening, zeros, *y*-intercept, and optimal values

• writing quadratic relation in standard form, factored form, and vertex form

• writing equations to model parabolas

• solving problems using quadratic equations

My Notes:

_____

_____

_____

_____

_____

_____

_____

_____

_____

Chapter 2

Knowledge and Understanding

Circle the correct answers.

① Which is not always present in a parabola?

    A. axis of symmetry   B. optimal value

    C. vertex   D. zeros

② If the second differences of a quadratic relation is _____ , then the direction of opening is _____ .

    A. positive ; upward   B. negative ; downward

    C. negative ; upward   D. A and B

③ Which quadratic equation does not have a maximum value?

    A. $y = -(x + 4)^2 + 2$ B. $y = -2(x - 5)^2 - 1$

    C. $y = 0.5x^2 - 4x + 8$ D. $y = -3x^2 + 2x - 10$

④ A quadratic relation in which form can have its zeros determined easily by inspection?

    A. standard form   B. factored form

    C. vertex form   D. all of the above

⑤ Which pair of zeros is not possible for its parabola to have an axis of symmetry at $x = 1$?

    A. -4 and 2   B. -1 and 3

    C. 0 and 2   D. -8 and 10

⑥ What is the vertex of the parabola $y = -3(x + 4)^2 - 8$?

    A. (4,8)   B. (-4,8)

    C. (4,-8)   D. (-4,-8)

⑦ How many zeros does $y = -2x(x + 4)$ have?

    A. 0   B. 1

    C. 2   D. more than 2

⑧ What is the y-intercept of the parabola $y = 4(x + 1)^2 - 7$?

    A. -7   B. 7

    C. -3   D. 3

Complete the table.

⑨

	y-intercept	zero(s)	vertex	direction of opening	axis of symmetry	optimal value	max. or min.
$y = -x(x - 2)$		0 and 2					
$y = (x - 2)(x + 4)$	-8						
$y = -(x + 4)^2 - 5$							
$y = 2x^2 + 4x + 5$		none					
$y = \frac{1}{5}(x + 5)^2 + 1$							

Determine the features of each quadratic relation by inspection. Then match it with the sketch of its graph. Write the letter.

⑩ a. $y = (x - 3)(x + 1)$

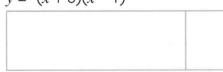

b. $y = (x + 1)^2 + 4$

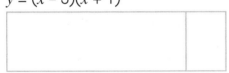

c. $y = 2x^2 + x + 3$

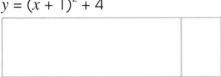

d. $y = -(x + 3)(x - 1)$

e. $y = \frac{1}{2}x^2 + 2x - 5$

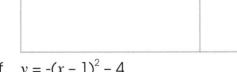

f. $y = -(x - 1)^2 - 4$

Ⓐ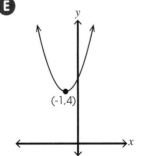

Ⓑ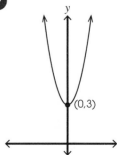

Ⓒ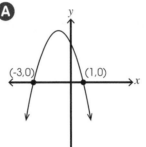

Ⓓ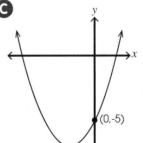

Ⓔ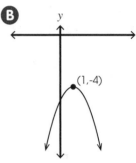

Ⓕ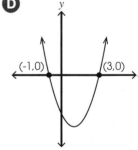

Write the quadratic relation for each graph in the indicated forms.

⑪ **A** vertex form: standard form:

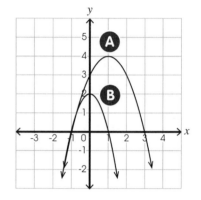

B factored form: vertex form:

Use the given information to find the quadratic relations in the specified forms.

⑫ vertex: (7,23)   point: (4,5)

vertex form:

⑬ zeros: 4, -2   vertex: (1,5)

factored form:

⑭ vertex: (-3,8)   y-intercept: -7

standard form:

⑮ zeros: -3, -1   minimum: -2

standard form:

For each scatter plot, use a curve of good fit to find the most reasonable equation. Write the letter.

⑯

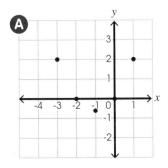

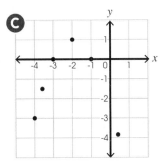

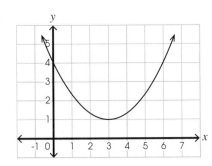

$y = 2(x - 1)^2 + 2$

$y = -(x + 3)(x + 1)$

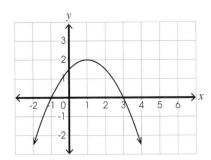

$y = \dfrac{2}{3}x^2 + \dfrac{4}{3}x$

Find an equation in the specified form for each curve.

⑰

vertex form:

⑱

factored form:

Find the answers.

⑲ A parabola has an axis of symmetry of $x = -5$ and one of its zeros is -2. Find the other zero.

_____

⑳ A parabola has a maximum of 6 and its zeros are 5 and -9. Find the vertex.

_____

㉑ A parabola has a y-intercept of -7 and no zeros. Its axis of symmetry is $x = -2$. Find another point that lies on the parabola.

_____

Solve the problems. Show your work.

㉒ A dolphin's jump resembles a parabolic curve. The height and horizontal distance travelled in metres are recorded.

Distance Travelled (m)	Height (m)
0	0
0.5	1
1	2
1.5	2.25
2	1.9
2.5	1.25
3	0

a. Plot the points and draw the curve of good fit.

b. Write an equation to model the curve.

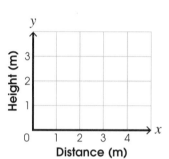

㉓ A football player threw the ball downfield. The path of the ball can be described using the equation $h = -0.01d^2 + 0.4d + 2$, where h is the height of the ball in metres and d is the distance downfield in metres.

a. What was the maximum height of the ball?

b. How far downfield did the ball land?

㉔ A deli sells 640 sandwiches per day at a price of $8 each. A marketing survey shows that for every $0.10 reduction in price, 40 more sandwiches will be sold. How much should the deli charge to maximize revenue? How many sandwiches will be sold at this price?

Communication

Answer the questions.

㉕ If a quadratic equation opens downward, what scenario will result in no zeros?

㉖ Describe the different ways of finding the axis of symmetry of a parabola in standard form, vertex form, and factored form.

Thinking

Answer the questions.

㉗ Imagine a parabolic arch that is 192 m wide and 192 m tall. Use an equation to model the arch where each x and y unit represents 1 m and the arch is symmetrical about the y-axis. Express the equation in vertex form.

㉘ Find the values of a and k so that the points (-5,-4) and (1,20) both lie on the parabola in the form $y = a(x + 3)^2 + k$.

Chapter 3

Transformations

3.1 Stretches/Compressions and Reflections

Key Ideas

In Chapter 2, you learned to identify the key features of quadratic relations, including the zeros, y-intercept, and vertex, in standard form, factored form, and vertex form.

In this chapter, you will learn to identify the parameters in a quadratic relation and use them to sketch a graph. Throughout this chapter, we will compare the graph of $y = x^2$ to those with different parameters.

Examples

Sketch the graphs of the relations based on the graph of $y = x^2$.

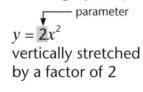

$y = 2x^2$
vertically stretched by a factor of 2

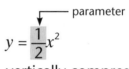

$y = \dfrac{1}{2}x^2$

vertically compressed

by a factor of $\dfrac{1}{2}$

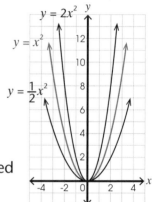

Complete the table of values of each quadratic relation. Match it with its graph. Then fill in the blanks to describe the graph compared to that of $y = x^2$.

Try these!

①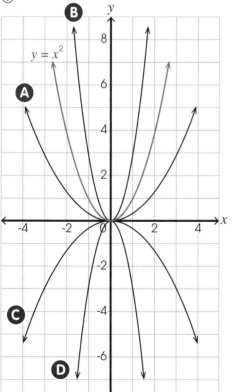

a.

x	y
-1	
0	
1	

$y = 3x^2$ ◯

vertically _____ by a factor

of _____

b.

x	y
-3	
0	
3	

$y = \dfrac{1}{3}x^2$ ◯

vertically _____ by a factor

of _____

c.

x	y
-1	
0	
1	

$y = -3x^2$ ◯

vertically _____ by a factor

of _____

d.

x	y
-3	
0	
3	

$y = -\dfrac{1}{3}x^2$ ◯

vertically _____ by a factor

of _____

Write the parameter, *a*, of each quadratic relation in the box.
Write whether the transformation is a stretch or a compression.
Then sketch it in relation to the given graph of $y = x^2$.

② $y = 4x^2$

③ $y = 0.2x^2$

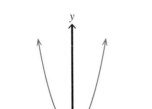

Hint

The value of *a* in the equation $y = ax^2$ determines whether its graph is a vertical stretch or a vertical compression.

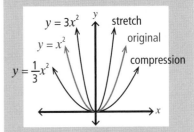

Consider the value of *a* in $y = ax^2$:

- if $a > 1$ or $a < -1$: vertical stretch

- if $-1 < a < 0$ or $0 < a < 1$: vertical compression

④ $y = 1.5x^2$

⑤ $y = 0.8x^2$

Write whether the graph of each quadratic relation opens upward or downward by examining the value of *a*. Then label the graphs.

Hint

The direction of opening can be determined by the value of *a*.

⑥ $y = 2x^2$ _____

$y = -x^2$ _____

⑦ $y = -\dfrac{1}{2}x^2$ _____

$y = \dfrac{1}{4}x^2$ _____

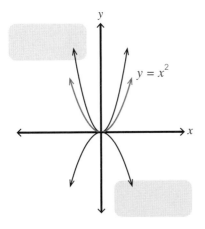

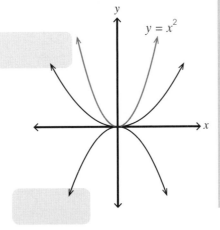

Consider the value of *a* in $y = ax^2$:

- if $a > 0$: opens upward
- if $a < 0$: opens downward

Circle the features of the relations and label their graphs. Then sketch the graphs.

⑧ a. $y = -4x^2$

- stretch / compression
- upward / downward

b. $y = 0.5x^2$

- stretch / compression
- upward / downward

c. $y = 0.1x^2$

- stretch / compression
- upward / downward

d. $y = -1.5x^2$

- stretch / compression
- upward / downward

⑨ Sketch the graphs of $y = -0.5x^2$ and $y = 4x^2$.

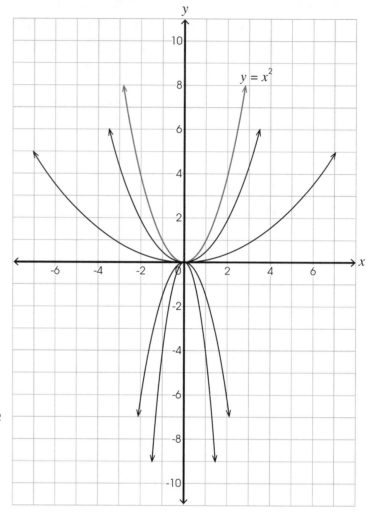

Write a quadratic relation that satisfies the description. Then sketch its graph.

⑩ • vertically stretched by a factor of 4
- opens upward

$y =$ _____

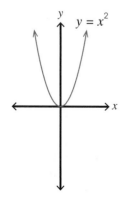

⑪ • vertically compressed by a factor of $\frac{1}{4}$
- opens downward

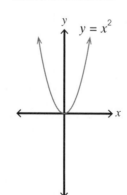

⑫ • vertically stretched by a factor of 2.5
- opens downward

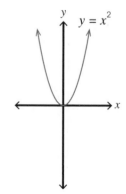

Answer the questions.

⑬ Match each quadratic relation with its graph in each group.

    a. $y = 1.8x^2$
        $y = 3.5x^2$
        $y = 0.4x^2$

    b. $y = 2.5x^2$
        $y = -2.5x^2$
        $y = -0.6x^2$

    c. $y = 0.7x^2$
        $y = -2.4x^2$
        $y = 0.2x^2$

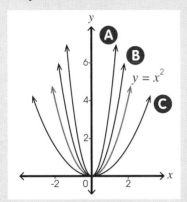
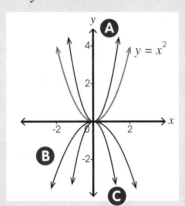
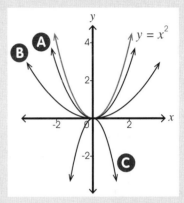

⑭ Sketch the graphs on the same grid by transforming the graph of $y = x^2$. Label all graphs.

    a. $y = -x^2$
    d. $y = 6x^2$

    b. $y = 3x^2$
    e. $y = -3.5x^2$

    c. $y = -0.1x^2$
    f. $y = 0.3x^2$

⑮ Find a possible value of a in $y = ax^2$ in order to produce each parabola using the given graphs.

    a.
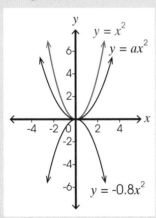

    b.
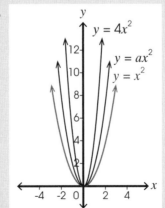

    c.
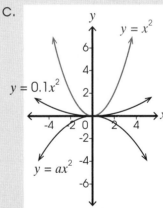

⑯ Write a quadratic relation for each parabola as described.

    a. Parabola A: vertically compressed by a factor of $\frac{1}{5}$ and opens upward in relation to $y = x^2$

    b. Parabola B: a reflection of Parabola A in the x-axis

    c. Parabola C: a reflection of Parabola B in the x-axis and vertically stretched by a factor of 10 of Parabola B

    d. Parabola D: wider than Parabola C and narrower than $y = x^2$; opens downward

Chapter 3

3.2 Translations

Key Ideas

In Chapter 3.1, you learned to stretch, compress, and reflect the parabola of $y = ax^2$ vertically in relation to $y = x^2$. In these transformations, the vertex stays at the origin (0,0).

Translations, on the other hand, change the location of the parabola by shifting it horizontally and/or vertically. Being able to identify the key parameters in a quadratic relation allows you to perform translations and sketch its graph.

Examples

Sketch the graphs of the relations.

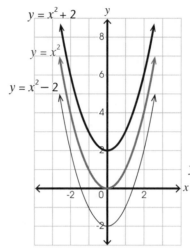

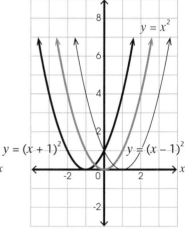

$y = x^2 + 2$ ⟵ translates 2 units up

$y = x^2 - 2$ ⟵ translates 2 units down

$y = (x - 1)^2$ ⟵ translates 1 unit right

$y = (x + 1)^2$ ⟵ translates 1 unit left

Complete the table of values to sketch each graph. Then fill in the blanks to describe the transformation.

① $y = x^2 + 1$

x	y
-2	
-1	
0	
1	
2	

$y = x^2 - 1$

x	y
-2	
-1	
0	
1	
2	

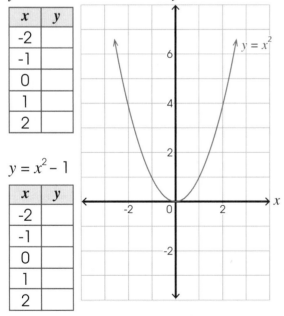

② $y = x^2 - 3$

x	y
-2	
-1	
0	
1	
2	

$y = x^2 + 3$

x	y
-2	
-1	
0	
1	
2	

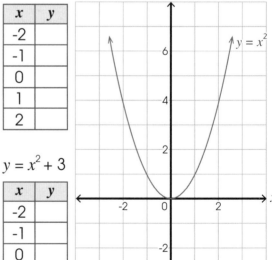

a. $y = x^2 + 1$: translates ☐ unit up

b. $y = x^2 - 1$: translates ☐ unit down

a. $y = x^2 - 3$: translates ☐ units

b. $y = x^2 + 3$: translates ☐ units

Identify the parameter which determines whether the graph of each relation translates up or down in relation to $y = x^2$. Then sketch the graph.

③ $y = x^2 + 4$

④ $y = x^2 - 4$

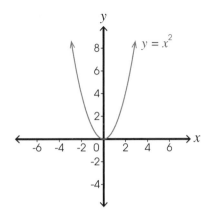

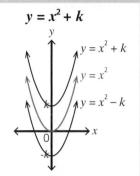
Complete the table of values of each relation. Graph and label it. Then describe the transformation.

⑤ $y = (x - 2)^2$

x	y
0	
2	
4	

$y = (x + 2)^2$

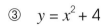

x	y
-4	
-2	
0	

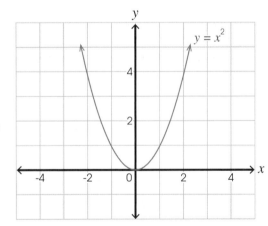

a. $y = (x - 2)^2$

translates _____

_____

b. $y = (x + 2)^2$

_____

_____

Determine whether the graph of each relation translates to the left or right. Then sketch the graph.

⑥ $y = (x - 3)^2$

⑦ $y = (x + 3)^2$

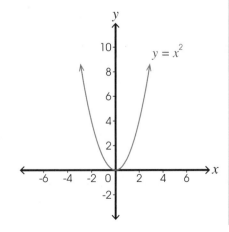

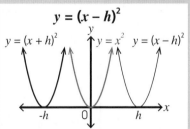

Complete the table of values and graph each relation. Find the vertex. Then answer the question.

⑧ $y = (x - 2)^2 + 1$

x	y
-1	
0	
1	
2	
3	
4	
5	

vertex

_____

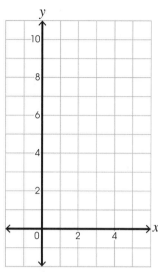

⑨ $y = (x + 1)^2 - 2$

x	y
-4	
-3	
-2	
-1	
0	
1	
2	

vertex

_____

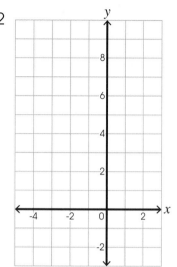

⑩ Relate the parameters, *h* and *k*, and the vertex of each relation. What do you find?

$y = (x - h)^2 + k$

translates left or right   translates up or down

_____

Identify and write the vertex of each relation. Then sketch its graph.

vertex

⑪ $y = (x + 2)^2 - 1$

_____

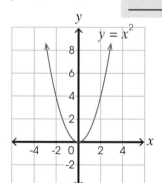

vertex

⑫ $y = (x - 2)^2 - 1$

_____

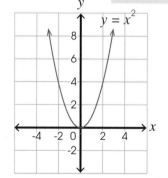

Hint

$y = (x - h)^2 + k$

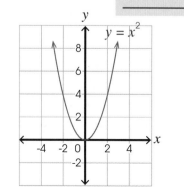

(h,k) is the vertex of $y = (x - h)^2 + k$.

vertex

⑬ $y = (x - 1)^2 + 2$

_____

⑭ $y = (x - 1)^2 - 2$

_____

Answer the questions.

⑮ The graph of $y = x^2$ is translated as shown. Find the quadratic relations of the translated graphs.

a.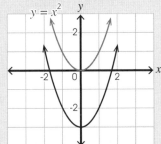

b.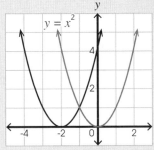

c.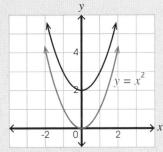

⑯ Match each quadratic relation with its graph.

a. $y = (x + 3)^2 - 1$

b. $y = (x + 3)^2 + 1$

c. $y = (x + 1)^2 + 3$

d. $y = (x - 1)^2 + 3$

e. $y = (x + 1)^2 - 3$

f. $y = (x - 3)^2 - 1$

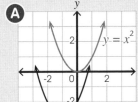
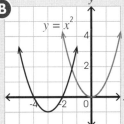
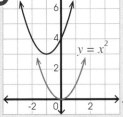

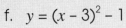
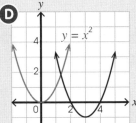
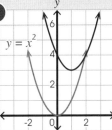

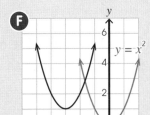

⑰ Describe the transformations of $y = x^2$ represented by each relation. Then sketch its graph. Make sure to start with the graph of $y = x^2$.

a. $y = x^2 - 5$

b. $y = (x + 4)^2$

c. $y = (x - 2)^2 + 4$

d. $y = (x + 3)^2 - 2$

Hint

The order of the transformations does not matter.

⑱ The graph of $y = x^2$ is translated as described below. Write the quadratic relation of each translated graph.

a. translated 5 units right and 1 unit down

b. translated 4 units left and 3 units up

M A T H   I R L

Quadratic equations are used by engineers of various fields. When developing equipment that has the resemblance of a curve, such as auto bodywork, quadratic equations are used to model them. Automobile engineers utilize quadratic equations to build the optimal brake system as well. Scan this QR code to learn more about the application of quadratic equations in different fields.

Chapter 3

3.3 Transformation with Vertex Form

Key Ideas

Recall the vertex form of quadratic relations you learned in Chapter 2.3.

Vertex Form

$$y = a(x - h)^2 + k$$

direction of opening — vertex: (h, k)

The values of the parameters, a, h, and k, allow us to sketch the parabola of any quadratic relation.

Examples

Sketch the graphs of the quadratic relations.

$y = 3(x + 2)^2 - 3$
- opens upward
- stretched by a factor of 3
- translates 2 units left and 3 units down

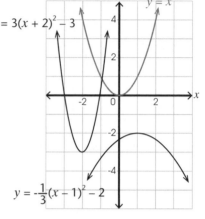

$y = -\dfrac{1}{3}(x - 1)^2 - 2$
- opens downward
- compressed by a factor of $\dfrac{1}{3}$
- translates 1 unit right and 2 units down

Complete the table of values and graph each relation. Then fill in the blanks to describe the transformations.

Try these!

① $y = 2(x - 1)^2 + 3$

x	y
-1	
0	
1	
2	
3	

- opens _____

- _____ by a factor of _____

- translates 1 unit _____ and
  _____ units up

② $y = -\dfrac{1}{4}(x + 2)^2 - 1$

x	y
-6	
-4	
-2	
0	
2	

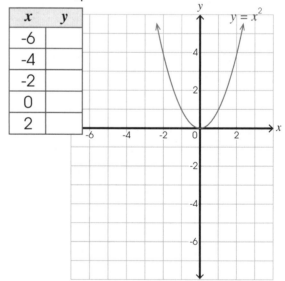

- opens _____

- _____ by a factor of _____

- translates _____ units _____
  and 1 unit _____

Describe the roles of the parameters in a quadratic relation.

③ **Parameter a**

stretch or compression

a. $a > 1$ or $a < -1$

_____

b. $0 < a < 1$ or $-1 < a < 0$

_____

direction of opening

c. $a > 0$

opens _____

d. $a < 0$

opens _____

④ **Parameter h**

left or right

a. $h > 0$

moves _____

b. $h < 0$

moves _____

⑤ **Parameter k**

up or down

a. $k > 0$

moves _____

b. $k < 0$

moves _____

vertex:
(___ , ___)

Hint

Vertex Form

$$y = a(x - h)^2 + k$$

vertex: (h, k)

- $a > 1$ or $a < -1$:
  vertical stretch

- $-1 < a < 0$ or $0 < a < 1$:
  vertical compression

- $a > 0$:
  opens upward

- $a < 0$:
  opens downward

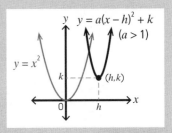

Identify the quadratic relation of each parabola. Write the letter.

⑥

a.

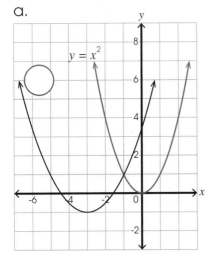

A $y = 2(x + 3)^2 - 1$

B $y = 0.5(x + 3)^2 - 1$

C $y = 0.1(x - 1)^2 - 3$

b.

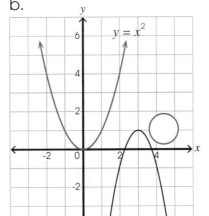

A $y = 2(x - 3)^2 + 1$

B $y = -3(x + 3)^2 + 1$

C $y = -2(x - 3)^2 + 1$

c.

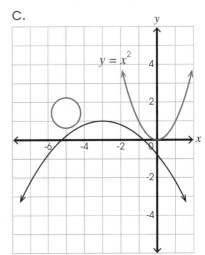

A $y = -0.2(x + 3)^2 + 1$

B $y = 2(x + 3)^2 + 1$

C $y = -0.5(x - 3)^2 + 1$

Sketch the parabola of each quadratic relation.

⑦ $y = -(x - 2)^2 + 1$

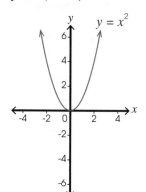

⑧ $y = 2(x + 3)^2 - 2$

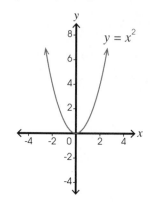

⑨ $y = -0.8(x - 3)^2 + 3$

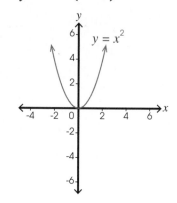

⑩ $y = -4(x - 2)^2 + 5$

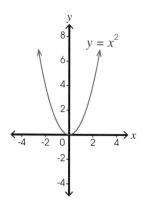

⑪ $y = -\dfrac{1}{3}(x - 1)^2 + 4$

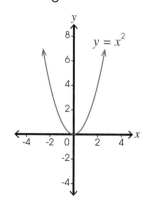

⑫ $y = 0.2x^2 + 2$

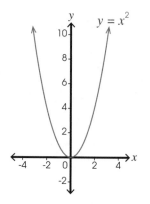

Check the possible quadratic relation of each parabola and complete the parameters.

⑬

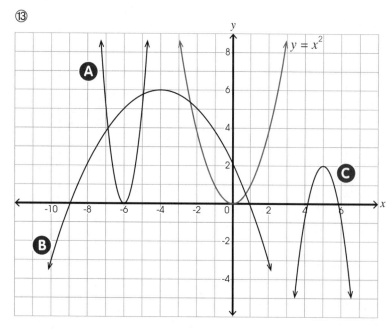

A

○ $y = 3x^2 - \boxed{}$

○ $y = 2(x - \boxed{})^2$

○ $y = 5(x + \boxed{})^2$

B

○ $y = 0.5(x + \boxed{})^2 + \boxed{}$

○ $y = -0.25(x + \boxed{})^2 + \boxed{}$

○ $y = -0.2(x - \boxed{})^2 + \boxed{}$

C

○ $y = -3(x - \boxed{})^2 + \boxed{}$

○ $y = 2(x - \boxed{})^2 + \boxed{}$

○ $y = -4(x + \boxed{})^2 + \boxed{}$

Answer the questions.

⑭ Match the relations with the parabolas.

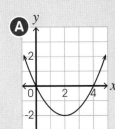 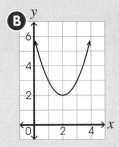

a. $y = (x - 2)^2 + 2$

b. $y = -(x + 2)^2 - 2$

c. $y = 0.5(x - 2)^2 - 2$

d. $y = -(x + 2)^2 + 2$

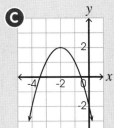 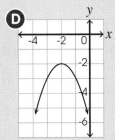

Things I have learned in this chapter:

• examining the parameter, a, in $y = ax^2$ to determine vertical stretches, compressions, and reflections

• examining the parameters, h and k, in $y = (x - h)^2 + k$ to determine horizontal and vertical translations

• sketching the graphs of quadratic relations by examining the parameters in vertex form

⑮ Find the quadratic relations described by the following transformations of $y = x^2$.

a. a parabola that is compressed vertically by a factor of $\frac{2}{5}$ and shifted 3 units left

b. a parabola that is stretched vertically by a factor of 9 and translated 4 units down

c. a parabola that opens downward and is moved 3 units up and has its axis of symmetry at $x = 3$

d. a parabola that is vertically compressed by a factor of $\frac{1}{2}$ with the vertex at (-2,4)

e. a parabola that is shifted half a unit down and 2 units right and reflected in the x-axis

⑯ Sketch the parabolas of the quadratic relations.

a. $y = \frac{1}{4}(x - 1)^2 + 2$

b. $y = 2(x + 3)^2 - 2$

c. $y = -\frac{1}{2}(x + 1)^2 - 4$

d. $y = -\frac{3}{2}(x - 3)^2 + 2$

⑰ Convert the quadratic relations from standard form to vertex form. Then sketch the graphs.

a. $y = 3x^2 + 12x + 6$

b. $y = \frac{1}{3}x^2 - 2x + 5$

Hint

Refer to Chapter 2.3 for conversions between the standard form and vertex form.

My Notes:

_____

_____

_____

_____

_____

_____

_____

_____

Knowledge and Understanding

Circle the correct answers.

① The parabola of which relation is a vertical stretch of the graph $y = x^2$?

    A. $y = 0.5(x - 1)^2 + 3$ B. $y = (x - 3)^2 + 1$

    C. $y = -3x^2 + 1$ D. $y = -(x - 1)^2 - 3$

② The parabola of which relation has its vertex at (1,-3)?

    A. $y = 0.5(x - 1)^2 + 3$ B. $y = (x - 3)^2 + 1$

    C. $y = -3x^2 + 1$ D. $y = -(x - 1)^2 - 3$

③ The graph of $y = x^2$ is reflected in the x-axis and then translated 2 units up and 3 units right. Which is the quadratic relation of the new parabola?

    A. $y = -(x - 3)^2 + 2$ B. $y = -(x + 3)^2 - 2$

    C. $y = -(x + 3)^2 + 2$ D. $y = (x - 3)^2 + 2$

④ Which statement is true about the graphs of $y = 2(x - 5)^2 + 2$ and $y = 2(x + 5)^2 + 2$?

    A. One graph has a vertex that is a minimum and the other is a maximum.

    B. The graphs have different shapes with different vertices.

    C. The graphs have the same shape with different vertices.

    D. The vertices are maximums.

⑤ Consider the graph as shown.

    a. Which equation represents the graph?

        A. $y = -(x + 3)^2 - 3$

        B. $y = -\dfrac{1}{3}(x - 3)^2 + 3$

        C. $y = -2(x - 3)^2 + 3$

        D. $y = \dfrac{1}{2}(x - 3)^2 + 3$

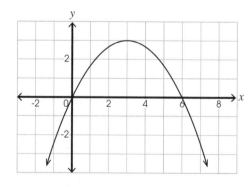

    b. The graph of which relation is compressed vertically of the one shown in the graph?

        A. $y = \dfrac{1}{3}(x - 3)^2 + 3$ B. $y = -\dfrac{1}{2}(x - 3)^2 + 3$

        C. $y = 3(x - 3)^2 + 3$ D. $y = -\dfrac{1}{8}(x - 3)^2 + 3$

Check the quadratic relation of each parabola.

⑥

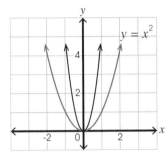

- Ⓐ $y = 5x^2$
- Ⓑ $y = -5x^2$

⑦

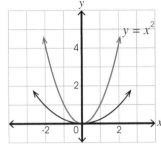

- Ⓐ $y = \frac{1}{4}x^2$
- Ⓑ $y = 4x^2$

⑧

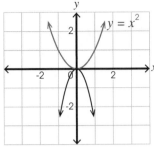

- Ⓐ $y = -3x^2$
- Ⓑ $y = 2x^2$

⑨

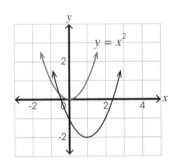

- Ⓐ $y = (x + 1)^2 - 2$
- Ⓑ $y = (x - 1)^2 - 2$

⑩

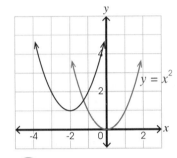

- Ⓐ $y = (x - 2)^2 + 1$
- Ⓑ $y = (x + 2)^2 + 1$

⑪

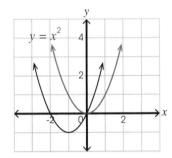

- Ⓐ $y = (x + 1)^2 - 1$
- Ⓑ $y = (x + 1)^2 + 1$

Match the parabolas with the quadratic relations.

⑫

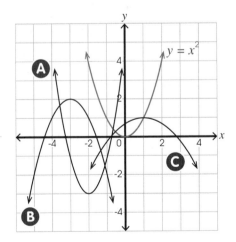

- ◯ $y = -(x + 3)^2 + 2$
- ◯ $y = 2(x + 2)^2 - 3$
- ◯ $y = -\frac{1}{3}(x - 1)^2 + 1$

⑬

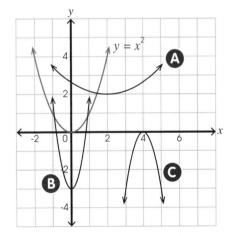

- ◯ $y = 5x^2 - 3$
- ◯ $y = -3(x - 4)^2$
- ◯ $y = \frac{1}{6}(x - 2)^2 + 2$

Describe the transformations applied to $y = x^2$ to obtain the graph of each quadratic relation.

⑭ $y = 3x^2 + 9$

⑮ $y = -\dfrac{1}{3}x^2 + 4$

⑯ $y = (x + 7)^2 + 2$

⑰ $y = 5(x - 3)^2 - 9$

⑱ $y = -\dfrac{5}{8}(x + 2)^2 - 1$

⑲ $y = -(x - \dfrac{1}{2})^2 + \dfrac{4}{3}$

The transformations are applied to the parabola of $y = x^2$. Determine the quadratic relations and answer the questions about them.

⑳
- translate 3 units left and 5 units up
- reflect in the x-axis

$y = $ _____

㉑
- vertically compressed by a factor of $\dfrac{1}{2}$
- shift 5 units right

㉒
- vertically stretched by a factor of 10
- translate 2 units down and 5 units left

㉓
- reflect in the x-axis
- vertically stretched by a factor of 3
- translate 5 units down

㉔ Which of the above quadratic relations

a. have a maximum? _____

b. has its vertex on the x-axis? _____

c. has its vertex on the y-axis? _____

d. has the same shape as the parabola of $y = x^2$? _____

e. is stretched most vertically? _____

f. has the axis of symmetry of $x = -5$? _____

Sketch the graphs of the quadratic relations.

㉕ $y = 3(x - 3)^2 + 1$

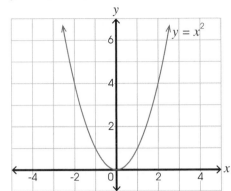

㉖ $y = -\dfrac{1}{4}(x + 2)^2 - 2$

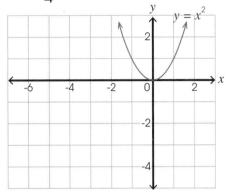

㉗ $y = -x^2 + 5$

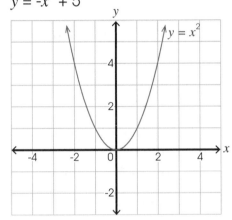

㉘ $y = -4(x + 3)^2 + 3$

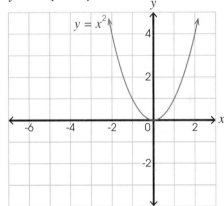

Convert the quadratic relations into vertex form. Then sketch the graphs and label them.

㉙ $y = 2x^2 + 8x + 10$

㉚ $y = -\dfrac{1}{2}x^2 + 4x - 8$

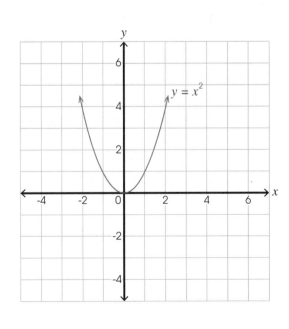

Write "T" for the true statements and "F" for the false ones.

③① The value of a in the equation $y = ax^2$ determines whether its graph is a vertical stretch or compression.

_____

③② For any value of k, the vertex of the parabola of the equation $y = x^2 + k$ must lie on the y-axis.

_____

③③ Consider the parabola of the equation $y = (x - h)^2$ for any value of h. The x-coordinate of the vertex must be 0.

_____

③④ For any value of a, h, and k, the parabolas of the equations $y = a(x - h)^2 + k$ and $y = a(x - h)^2 - k$ must be reflections of each other in the y-axis.

_____

Application

Solve the problems.

③⑤ A swimmer dived into a pool. The depth he reached at time x in seconds is y in metres. It is given by $y = 1.5(x - 2)^2 - 6$.

a. Sketch a graph to illustrate the scenario.

b. How deep did the swimmer reach?

c. How long did it take the swimmer to reach the deepest point?

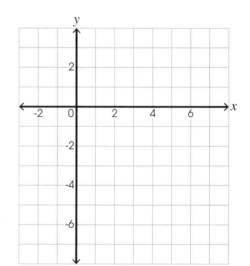

③⑥ Andrew kicked a ball. The height of the ball at time x in seconds is y in metres. It is given by $y = -5(x - 1)^2 + 5$.

a. Sketch a graph to illustrate the scenario.

b. What was the maximum height the ball reached?

c. How long did it take the ball to reach the maximum height?

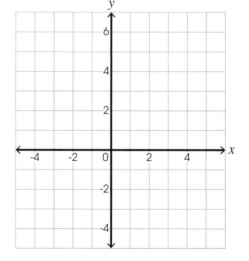

Communication

Answer the questions.

㊲ Given $y = a(x - h)^2 + k$, describe the parabola and its transformations from the graph of $y = x^2$.

   a. $a < -1$ b. $0 < a < 1$ c. $a > 1$

㊳ Describe how the number of zeros of a quadratic relation in the form $y = a(x - h)^2 + k$ can be determined by the values of the parameters.

Thinking

Find the answers.

㊴ The parabola of $y = x^2$ is transformed and the new parabola lies on (7,12). Determine two possible sets of transformations and find the equations of the new parabola.

㊵ Determine the values of a and b in the relation $y = ax^2 + bx + 12$ if the vertex is at (3,6).

Chapter 4

Quadratic Equations

4.1 Solving Quadratic Equations

Key Ideas

To solve a quadratic equation is to determine the zeros, also called roots, of the equation.

If a product of factors is zero, then at least one of the factors must be zero.

e.g. $4a = 0$ $xy = 0$

   a must be 0. x or y must be 0.

Follow the steps below to solve quadratic equations.

❶ Express the equation in factored form $a(x - r)(x - s) = 0$.

❷ Set the factor(s) to zero and solve for x.

   $x - r = 0$ or $x - s = 0$

   $x = r$ $x = s$

Examples

Solve the quadratic equations.

$x^2 - x - 6 = 0$

$(x - 3)(x + 2) = 0$ ← factored; either $(x - 3)$ or $(x + 2)$ is 0

$x - 3 = 0$ or $x + 2 = 0$

   $x = 3$ $x = -2$

So, the roots are 3 and -2.

$2x^2 + 7x + 3 = 0$

$(2x + 1)(x + 3) = 0$ ← factored

$2x + 1 = 0$ or $x + 3 = 0$

   $x = -\dfrac{1}{2}$ $x = -3$

So, the roots are $-\dfrac{1}{2}$ and -3.

Try these!

Fill in the blanks to solve the quadratic equations.

① $\qquad x^2 + 3x + 2 = 0$

$(x + \boxed{})(x + \boxed{}) = 0$ ← rewriting the equation in factored form

$x + \boxed{} = 0$ or $x + \boxed{} = 0$ ← setting the factors to 0

$x = \boxed{}$ $x = \boxed{}$

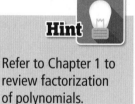

Hint

Refer to Chapter 1 to review factorization of polynomials.

② $\qquad 2x^2 + 5x + 2 = 0$

$(2x + \boxed{})(x + \boxed{}) = 0$

$2x + \boxed{} = 0$ or $x + \boxed{} = 0$

$x = \boxed{}$ $x = \boxed{}$

③ $\qquad 2x^2 - 5x + 2 = 0$

$(2x - \boxed{})(x - \boxed{}) = 0$

$2x - \boxed{} = 0$ or $x - \boxed{} = 0$

$x = \boxed{}$ $x = \boxed{}$

Solve the equations by factoring. Show your work.

④ $x^2 + 5x + 4 = 0$

⑤ $x^2 + 6x = 0$

Hint

Factors without a variable do not lead to a root.

3 does not lead to a root.

e.g. $3(x + 1)(x - 1) = 0$

$x + 1 = 0$ or $x - 1 = 0$
$x = -1$ $x = 1$

Equations with the square of the same factor lead to only one root.

e.g. $(x + 2)^2 = 0$
$x + 2 = 0$
$x = -2$

⑥ $x^2 + x - 6 = 0$

⑦ $x^2 - 5x - 24 = 0$

⑧ $2x^2 + 7x + 6 = 0$

⑨ $3x^2 + 15x + 12 = 0$

⑩ $4x^2 + 10x + 4 = 0$

⑪ $x^2 + 10x + 25 = 0$

⑫ $8x^2 - 8x + 2 = 0$

Solve the equations. Show your work.

⑬ $x^2 + 4x - 1 = 4$

⑭ $x^2 - 3x - 2 = 8$

Hint

Remember to rearrange the terms in each equation to make the equation equal to zero before factoring.

subtract 3 from

e.g. $x^2 - 3x - 1 = 3$ ← both sides; make it equal to 0

$x^2 - 3x - 4 = 0$ ← can be solved by factoring

⑮ $3x^2 + 2x + 1 = 2$

⑯ $4x^2 - 6x + 1 = -1$

⑰ $3x^2 - 6x = -3$

Solve the quadratic equations. Check your answers. Show your work.

⑱ $2x^2 + 3x - 14 = 0$

⑲ $3x^2 + 11x = -6$

Check

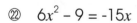

$2()^2 + 3() - 14 = $

$2()^2 + 3() - 14 = $

Check

⑳ $2x^2 + 6 = 7x$

㉑ $-10x^2 - 6 = -32x$

Check

Check

㉒ $6x^2 - 9 = -15x$

㉓ $9x^2 + 4 = -12x$

Check

Check

Simplify each equation and solve. Show your work.

㉔ $(x + 1)^2 = 16$

㉕ $x^2 - x - 6 = -6 - 7x$

㉖ $3x^2 = 2(5x + 4)$

㉗ $4x(x + 5) + 13 = 3(x + 30)$

㉘ $10x^2 + 2x - 73 = (x + 1)(9x - 1)$

㉙ $4x^2 + 10x + 8 = -(x + 2)(2x - 1)$

Answer the questions.

㉚ Determine whether the given value is a root of the quadratic equation.

a. $x = 5$ and $2x^2 + 9x - 5 = 0$

b. $x = \dfrac{3}{2}$ and $2x^2 + 5x - 12 = 0$

㉛ Write a quadratic equation in standard form with the given roots.

a. 3 and 5

b. 0 and $\dfrac{1}{3}$

Use the given graph to find the zeros of each equation. Then solve the equation algebraically and answer the questions.

③②

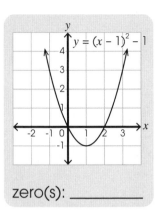

$(x - 1)^2 - 1 = 0$

Hint

The zeros of the graphs are the x-intercepts. They are also the roots of the equations when $y = 0$.

zero(s): _____   root(s): _____

③③

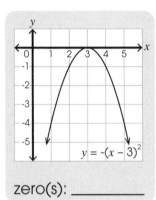

zero(s): _____

$-(x - 3)^2 = 0$

③④

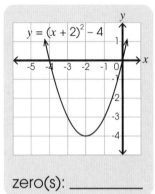

zero(s): _____

$(x + 2)^2 - 4 = 0$

③⑤

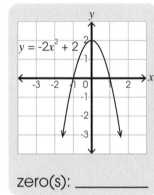

zero(s): _____

$-2x^2 + 2 = 0$

root(s): _____   root(s): _____   root(s): _____

③⑥ Compare the zeros of the graphs and the roots of the corresponding equations. What do you find?

_____

_____

③⑦ Selena wants to solve $7x^2 + 11x - 9 = 0$ using a graphing calculator. What should she look for to find the solution?

_____

_____

Answer the questions.

㊳ Find the root(s) of the quadratic equations.

a. $(x + 2)(x - 1) = 0$ b. $(x + 3)(x + 4) = 0$

c. $(x - 5)(x - 2) = 0$ d. $(2x + 1)(x - 3) = 0$

e. $(x + 1)(3x - 2) = 0$ f. $(5x + 1)(2x + 5) = 0$

g. $2(x + 1)(2x + 7) = 0$ h. $-(x - 6)(3x + 1) = 0$

i. $-3(x + 8)(4x - 3) = 0$ j. $-5(2x + 5)(4x - 1) = 0$

㊴ Solve the equations by factoring.

a. $x^2 - 13x + 42 = 0$ b. $x^2 - 8x - 48 = 0$

c. $x^2 + 8x + 15 = 0$ d. $3x^2 - 5x - 8 = 0$

e. $8x^2 + 2x - 15 = 0$ f. $4x^2 + 15x - 4 = 0$

g. $9x^2 - 45x = 0$ h. $2x^2 - 128 = 0$

i. $8x^2 + 13x + 5 = 0$ j. $14x^2 - 49x - 63 = 0$

㊵ Solve the quadratic equations using a graphing calculator.

a. $y = (x + 2)^2$ b. $y = -(x + 1)^2 + 4$

c. $y = 2(x - 3)^2 - 8$ d. $y = x^2 + 10x + 24$

㊶ Solve the equations algebraically.

a. $x^2 = x + 2$ b. $2x^2 = 40 - 11x$

c. $14x^2 - 5 = 33x$ d. $3x^2 + 36x + 49 = 8x$

e. $4x^2 - 77 = -17x$ f. $6x(x - 3) - 18 = 6$

㊷ Check whether each value is a root in the quadratic equation.

a. $x = 6$ and $x^2 - 2x - 6 = 0$ b. $x = -3$ and $2x^2 + 5x - 3 = 0$

c. $x = -\dfrac{1}{2}$ and $2x^2 + 9x - 5 = 0$ d. $x = \dfrac{3}{4}$ and $16x^2 - 9 = 0$

㊸ Write a quadratic equation in standard form with the given root(s).

a. 4 and -1   b. -7 and -2

c. $\dfrac{1}{6}$ and $\dfrac{1}{3}$ d. $\dfrac{4}{5}$

e. 2 and $-1\dfrac{2}{3}$ f. -2.5 and -4.5

㊹ Thomas says, "If two quadratic equations have the same roots, then they must also have the same axis of symmetry and direction of opening." Is he correct? Explain.

㊺ Describe a scenario where a quadratic equation has solutions but cannot be solved by factoring.

㊻ Jenny says, "The quadratic equation $x^2 - 3x + 1 = 0$ is not factorable, so it must not have a solution." Is she correct? Explain.

Chapter 4

4.2 Quadratic Formula

Key Ideas

Not all quadratic equations can be solved by factoring, but that does not mean that they are not solvable.

The quadratic formula can be used to determine the roots of a quadratic equation in the form $ax^2 + bx + c = 0$.

Quadratic Formula

$$x = \frac{-b \pm \sqrt{b^2 - 4ac}}{2a}$$

To apply the quadratic formula, first determine the coefficients, a and b, and the constant, c, in the equation.

The $\pm$ symbol in the formula implies that there will be two solutions, one by addition and the other by subtraction.

Examples

Solve using the quadratic formula.

$x^2 - 5x - 14 = 0$ ← $a = 1$, $b = -5$, $c = -14$

$x = \dfrac{-b \pm \sqrt{b^2 - 4ac}}{2a}$

$x = \dfrac{-(-5) \pm \sqrt{(-5)^2 - 4(1)(-14)}}{2(1)}$

$x = \dfrac{5 \pm \sqrt{25 + 56}}{2}$

$x = \dfrac{5 \pm \sqrt{81}}{2}$

$x = \dfrac{5 \pm 9}{2}$ ← The $\pm$ symbol denotes both addition and subtraction.

$x = \dfrac{5 + 9}{2}$ or $x = \dfrac{5 - 9}{2}$

$x = 7$ $\qquad x = -2$

So, the roots are 7 and -2.

Write the correct values of a, b, and c. Then check the correct application of the quadratic formula.

Try these!

① $x^2 - 2x + 3 = 0$

$a = \boxed{}$ $\quad b = \boxed{}$ $\quad c = \boxed{}$

(A) $x = \dfrac{-2 \pm \sqrt{2^2 - 4(1)(3)}}{2(1)}$

(B) $x = \dfrac{-(-2) \pm \sqrt{(-2)^2 - 4(1)(3)}}{2(1)}$

② $-x^2 + 5x - 4 = 0$

$a = \boxed{}$ $\quad b = \boxed{}$ $\quad c = \boxed{}$

(A) $x = \dfrac{-5 \pm \sqrt{5^2 - 4(-1)(-4)}}{2(-1)}$

(B) $x = \dfrac{5 \pm \sqrt{(-1)^2 - 4(5)(-4)}}{2(1)}$

③ $2x^2 - 3x + 4 = 0$

$a = \boxed{}$ $\quad b = \boxed{}$ $\quad c = \boxed{}$

(A) $x = \dfrac{3 \pm \sqrt{(-3)^2 - 4(2)(4)}}{2(-3)}$

(B) $x = \dfrac{-(-3) \pm \sqrt{(-3)^2 - 4(2)(4)}}{2(2)}$

④ $-5x^2 + x = 0$

$a = \boxed{}$ $\quad b = \boxed{}$ $\quad c = \boxed{}$

(A) $x = \dfrac{-1 \pm \sqrt{1^2 - 4(-5)}}{2(-5)}$

(B) $x = \dfrac{-1 \pm \sqrt{1^2 - 4(-5)(0)}}{2(-5)}$

Solve using the quadratic formula. Show your work.

⑤ $x^2 + 4x + 3 = 0$

$$x = \frac{-\boxed{} \pm \sqrt{\boxed{}^2 - 4(\boxed{})(\boxed{})}}{2(\boxed{})}$$

$$x = \frac{\boxed{} \pm \sqrt{\boxed{}}}{\boxed{}} \quad \longleftarrow \quad x = \frac{\boxed{} + \boxed{}}{\boxed{}} = \boxed{} \quad \text{or} \quad x = \frac{\boxed{} - \boxed{}}{\boxed{}} = \boxed{}$$

⑥ $x^2 + 3x - 4 = 0$

⑦ $-x^2 - 10x - 9 = 0$

⑧ $2x^2 + 3x - 2 = 0$

⑨ $2x^2 - 4x - 6 = 0$

Hint

Simplifying an equation before solving it makes the calculations easier.

e.g. $2x^2 + 4x - 10 = 0$

$2(x^2 + 2x - 5) = 0$

apply quadratic formula

⑩ $4x^2 - 8x + 3 = 0$

⑪ $3x^2 + 21x + 18 = 0$

Solve the quadratic equations. Round your answers to two decimal places if needed.

⑫ $4x^2 + 25 = -20x$

⑬ $x(3x - 8) = -1$

Hint

Rearrange the terms and simplify to express the equations in standard form before solving.

⑭ $4 - 5x^2 = 5(x + 1)$

⑮ $13x + 10x^2 + 2 = 1 + 5x + 3x^2$

⑯ $(x - 2)(x - 6) = 3x(x + 1)$

⑰ $x(x + 1) = -4x(x - 3)$

⑱ $(x - 2)^2 = 5x^2$

⑲ $(2x + 1)^2 = -(5x + 4)^2 + 2$

Use the quadratic formula to find the *x*-intercepts of the quadratic equations. Round the answers to two decimal places if needed. Then label the graphs.

⑳ $y = x^2 - 2x - 1$

㉑ $y = x^2 + 6x + 7$

Hint

Set *y* to 0 and solve.

㉒ $y = 2x^2 + x - 2$

㉓ $y = -x^2 + 7x - 9$

㉔ $y = 3x^2 - 4x - 3$

㉕ $y = -4x^2 - 2x$

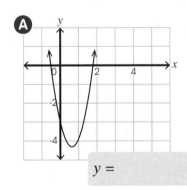

(A) $y =$

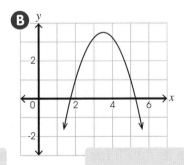

(B)

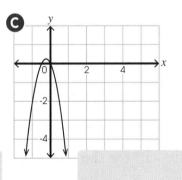

(C)

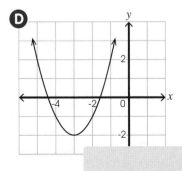

(D)

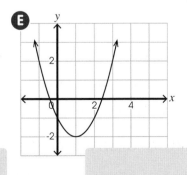

(E)

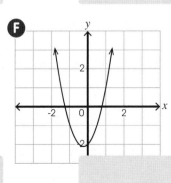

(F)

Solve each quadratic equation by factoring and by using the quadratic formula. Then answer the questions.

㉖ $x^2 - 18x + 81 = 0$

> [by factoring]
>
>
>
> [using quadratic formula]

㉗ $-4x^2 + 8x - 3 = 0$

> [by factoring]
>
>
>
> [using quadratic formula]

㉘ Under what circumstances would you prefer factoring over using the quadratic formula to solve a quadratic equation?

_____

_____

㉙ If a quadratic equation cannot be factored, what strategies can be used to solve it?

_____

_____

Write "T" for the true statements and "F" for the false ones.

㉚ The quadratic formula can only be applied to quadratic equations that cannot be factored. _____

㉛ The quadratic formula is applied to solve a quadratic equation in the form $ax^2 + bx + c = 0$.

a. The solution of a quadratic equation cannot be found if $a = 0$. _____

b. The solution of a quadratic equation cannot be found if $b = 0$. _____

c. The solution of a quadratic equation cannot be found if $b^2 - 4ac < 0$. _____

Answer the questions.

③② Find the roots using the quadratic equation. Give exact answers.

a. $x^2 + 5x + 4 = 0$

b. $x^2 - x - 6 = 0$

c. $-x^2 + 2x + 3 = 0$

d. $-x^2 - 7x - 6 = 0$

e. $2x^2 - 9x + 7 = 0$

f. $3x^2 - 8x + 4 = 0$

g. $4x^2 - x - 2 = 0$

h. $3x^2 - 6x + 1 = 0$

③③ Solve the equations. Round your answers to two decimal places if needed.

a. $8x^2 = -5 + 14x$

b. $9x^2 - 3 = 8x$

c. $18x^2 + 51x = 42$

d. $4x^2 - 2.5x - 5.3 = 0$

e. $2x(x + 2) = 48$

f. $(2x + 5)(2x - 5) = -(x + 3)^2$

③④ Find the x-intercepts of the graphs of the quadratic relations using the quadratic formula. Then do the matching.

a. $y = -x^2 + 3x + 3$

b. $y = -\frac{1}{2}x^2 - 2x - 1$

c. $y = 0.8x^2 - 4x + 1$

d. $y = 2.5x^2 - 6.5x + 1$

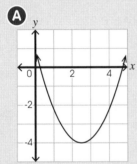 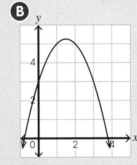 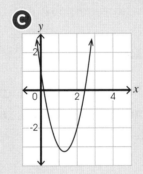 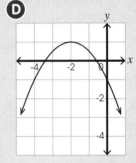

③⑤ Compare the advantages and disadvantages of solving a quadratic equation by factoring and by using the quadratic formula.

Hint

Refer to Chapter 2.3 on converting from standard form into vertex form.

③⑥ Robert says, "I tried to use the quadratic formula to solve for $x^2 + 4x + 6 = 0$ but I got an error message on my calculator."

a. Convert the equation into vertex form. Identify the vertex of the graph and its direction of opening.

b. Explain why Robert got an error when using the quadratic formula.

Hint

③⑦ Determine the points of intersection of the line $y = 2x - 3$ and the parabola $y = 2x^2 + 5x - 2$ algebraically.

Substitute the value of y of the linear equation into the y of the quadratic equation.

Chapter 4

4.3   Real Roots and Discriminants

Key Ideas

A quadratic expression may have 0, 1, or 2 real roots*. We can determine the number of roots by finding the discriminant.

$D = b^2 - 4ac$ ← discriminant: an expression in the quadratic formula

$D > 0$	$D = 0$	$D < 0$
2 real roots	1 real root	0 real roots
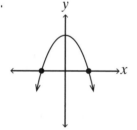		
• 2 distinct zeros	• 1 zero	• no zeros

*Real roots are real numbers. Notably, the square roots of negative integers are not real numbers.

Examples

Find the discriminants to determine the number of real roots.

$x^2 - 5x + 4 = 0$ ← $a = 1, b = -5, c = 4$

$D = b^2 - 4ac$
$ = (-5)^2 - 4(1)(4)$
$ = 25 - 16$
$ = 9$

Since $D > 0$, there are 2 real roots.

$-5x^2 + 3x - 1 = 0$ ← $a = -5, b = 3, c = -1$

$D = b^2 - 4ac$
$ = 3^2 - 4(-5)(-1)$
$ = 9 - 20$
$ = -11$

Since $D < 0$, there are no real roots.

Write ">", "<", or "=" to complete the discriminant based on the graph. Then find the number of real roots based on the given discriminants.

Try these!

① a.

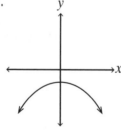

$D \quad\boxed{}\quad 0$

b.

$D \quad\boxed{}\quad 0$

②

Discriminant	Number of Real Roots
a. $D = 5$	_____
b. $D = 0$	_____
c. $D = -1$	_____
d. $D = -3$	_____
e. $D = 2.5$	_____
f. $D = -0.1$	_____

c.

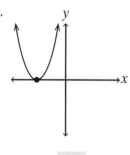

$D \quad\boxed{}\quad 0$

d.

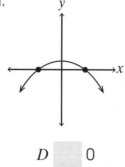

$D \quad\boxed{}\quad 0$

Find the discriminant and determine the number of real roots for each quadratic expression. Show your work.

③ $7x^2 - 9x + 2 = 0$

$D = b^2 - 4ac$

$= ()^2 - 4()()$

$= - $

$= $

_____ real roots

④ $2x^2 + 8x + 9 = 0$

Hint

The discriminant, $b^2 - 4ac$, is part of the quadratic formula.

$x = \dfrac{-b \pm \sqrt{b^2 - 4ac}}{2a}$ ← discriminant

When $D > 0$, $\sqrt{b^2 - 4ac}$ gives a real number. There are two distinct real roots.

When $D = 0$, $\sqrt{b^2 - 4ac}$ is zero. There is only one real root.

When $D < 0$, $\sqrt{b^2 - 4ac}$ cannot be evaluated because the square root of a negative number is not a real number. There are no real roots.

⑤ $6x^2 + 13x - 4 = 0$

⑥ $25x^2 - 10x + 1 = 0$

⑦ $3x^2 - 2x = -9$

⑧ $3x^2 - 8 = 0$

⑨ $x^2 + 7 = 4x + 1$

⑩ $2x^2 + 4(x + 1) = 2$

⑪ $(2x + 3)(x - 2) = -(x - 4)^2$

Determine the number of x-intercepts each quadratic equation has. Match it with its graph.

⑫ a. $y = x^2 + 2x - 3$

b. $y = 2x^2 - 5x + 8$

c. $y = 2x^2 - 8x + 8$

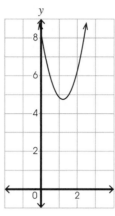 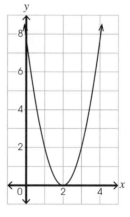 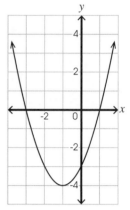

$y =$ _____ _____ _____

⑬ a. $y = -2x^2 + 2x - 1$

b. $y = -x^2 + 5x - 3$

c. $y = -0.5x^2 + 1.8x - 1.62$

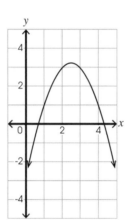 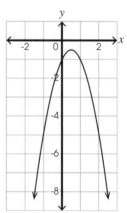 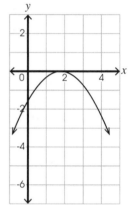

$y =$ _____ _____ _____

Answer the questions.

⑭ Find the value of k in each quadratic equation so that it has exactly one real root.

a. $x^2 - 16x + k = 0$ b. $3x^2 + kx + 12 = 0$

⑮ Determine the range of values that k can be in $kx^2 - 4x + 1 = 0$ if

a. there are two real roots.   b. there are no real roots.

Answer the questions.

⑯ Determine the number of real roots of a quadratic equation with each discriminant.

    a. $D = 4$ b. $D = -2$ c. $D = 0$ d. $D = -1$

⑰ Determine the discriminant for each quadratic equation as described below.

    a. The equation is a perfect-square trinomial.

    b. The vertex of its parabola is at $(1,1)$ and opens upward.

    c. The equation is in factored form.

⑱ Find the discriminant and the number of roots.

    a. $x^2 + 3x + 2 = 0$ b. $10x^2 - 6x + 1 = 0$

    c. $5x^2 - 10x + 5 = 0$ d. $9x^2 + 0.25 = 0$

⑲ Determine if each equation has real roots. If so, find the roots.

    a. $x^2 + 5x + 7 = 0$ b. $-x^2 + 3x + 10 = 0$

    c. $2x^2 - 4x + 2 = 0$ d. $5x^2 - 2x - 3 = 0$

⑳ Find the x-intercepts of the quadratic relations.

    a. $y = x^2 - 3x + 11$ b. $y = 8x^2 + 7x - 9$

    c. $y = x^2 - 2x + 5$ d. $y = 3x^2 - 6x + 2$

㉑ Determine the value of k in each quadratic equation so that there is only one real root.

    a. $x^2 + kx + 7 = 0$ b. $-4x^2 + 28x + k = 0$

    c. $kx^2 + 3x + 2 = 0$ d. $3kx^2 - 12x + 2 = 0$

㉒ Determine the range of values that k can be in $2x^2 - kx + 2 = 0$ with the given number of real roots.

    a. no real roots   b. one real root   c. two real roots

㉓ Use the discriminant to explain why perfect-square trinomials always have one real root.

㉔ Describe how you can use the discriminant to determine whether a quadratic relation has x-intercepts.

㉕ If a and b are non-zero real numbers, show that $(a - b)x^2 - 2ax + (a + b) = 0$ has two real roots.

㉖ Determine the number of points of intersection of the parabolas $y = 2x^2 + x - 1$ and $y = 3(x - 1)^2 + 2$. If there are any point(s) of intersection, determine their coordinates.

Chapter 4

Key Ideas

When solving word problems that involve quadratic equations, remember the tips below.

- Use a variable to represent the unknown. If there are multiple unknowns, choose one unknown and represent the rest in terms of the chosen one.
- Set up an equation based on the given information.
- If the maximum or minimum is to be determined, use the vertex form.
- If the zeros or roots are to be determined, either use the factored form if factorable or the standard form and apply the quadratic formula.
- Sometimes, even if there are two distinct real solutions, only one of them can be reasonable.

Examples

The sum of two numbers is 12. Their product is 35. Find the numbers.

Let x be one of the numbers and $(12 - x)$ be the other number.

$$x(12 - x) = 35$$
$$12x - x^2 = 35$$
$$x^2 - 12x + 35 = 0 \leftarrow \text{standard form}$$
$$(x - 7)(x - 5) = 0 \leftarrow \begin{array}{l}\text{goal: find the zeros;} \\ \text{convert into factored form}\end{array}$$
$$x - 7 = 0 \quad \text{or} \quad x - 5 = 0$$
$$x = 7 \qquad\qquad x = 5$$

If $x = 5$, then $12 - 5 = 7$.

If $x = 7$, then $12 - 7 = 5$.

So, the numbers are 5 and 7.

For each scenario, check the approach in finding the solution and the correct equation.

Try these!

① Two numbers have a difference of 8. The sum of their squares is 130. Find the numbers.

  a. Goal:

     Ⓐ finding the maximum/minimum

     Ⓑ finding the zeros

  b. Equation:

     Ⓐ $x^2 + (x + 8)^2 = 130$

     Ⓑ $x^2 - (x - 8)^2 = 130$

     Ⓒ $x^2 + 8^2 = 130$

② 40 wood panels are available to enclose a rectangular field. What dimensions will create the greatest area?

  a. Goal:

     Ⓐ finding the maximum/minimum

     Ⓑ finding the zeros

  b. Equation:

     Ⓐ $A = l(20 - l)$

     Ⓑ $A = 2l + 2w$

     Ⓒ $A = l(40 - l)$

Solve the problems. Show your work.

③ The equation $h = -5t^2 + 20t + 25$ gives the approximate height, h, in metres, of a Frisbee thrown over time, t, in seconds. What was the Frisbee's maximum height?

④ A ball was thrown and its path is described by $h = -5t^2 + 10t$, where h is the height in metres and t is the time in seconds. How long was the ball in the air?

⑤ A dance team wants to create costumes for a performance. The cost of the costumes is modelled by $C = 0.1x^2 + 2.4x + 5$, where C is the total cost and x is the number of costumes. How many costumes can they purchase for $453?

⑥ The area of a rectangular field is 2275 m². The field is enclosed by 200 m of fencing. What are the dimensions of the field?

⑦ Bill's business model shows the profit using $P = -0.003x^2 + 12x + 27\,760$, where P is the profit after x items sold. He aims to earn \$40 000 this year. Find the discriminant to determine whether this is possible.

⑧ A lunch cruise charges \$36 per passenger and it averages 360 passengers per day. A survey determined that for every \$2 increase, the cruise will lose 10 passengers. Determine the maximum revenue.

⑨ A club sells T-shirts to raise money. Last year, they sold 1200 T-shirts for \$20 each. If they raised the price by \$2, 60 fewer T-shirts would be sold. If the club predicts that the revenue will be \$17 280 this year, at what price will they sell the T-shirts?

⑩ A rectangular lawn measures 30 m by 40 m and a landscaper mowed the lawn from the border inward. When the lawn is half-mowed, the width of the mowed strip is uniform around the border. How wide is the strip?

Answer the questions.

⑪ The length of a rectangle is 5 cm greater than twice the width. The area is 33 cm². What are its dimensions?

⑫ Determine two positive consecutive odd integers whose product is 323.

⑬ A ball was thrown up into the air from a building. Its height, h, in metres after t seconds was $h = -4.9t^2 + 38t + 110$. When did the ball reach the ground?

⑭ The path of a baseball thrown from a height of 1.5 m above ground is given by $h = -0.25d^2 + 2d + 1.5$, where h is the height in metres and d is the horizontal distance in metres. What was the maximum height of the baseball?

⑮ A candy store sells chocolates at $4 per kg. At this price, 300 kg of chocolates are sold each week. If every $0.10 increase in price results in 5 fewer kg sold, what price per kg will generate $1237.50 in total?

⑯ A building's rectangular base of 100 m by 80 m is to be surrounded by a lawn of uniform width. The area of the lawn must be equal to the base area of the building. Determine the width of the lawn to the nearest metre.

⑰ A photograph measuring 12 cm by 8 cm is to be mounted on a board to create a border of equal width all around. The area of the border is equal to that of the photograph. What are the dimensions of the border?

⑱ Is it possible for the sum of the squares of three positive consecutive integers to be 194? If so, what are the integers?

M A T H   I R L

Projectile motion is when an object moves under the effect of Earth's gravity. This type of motion is parabolic and can be modelled by quadratic relations. The variables involved include the force of gravity, the initial speed and height of the object, and time. Scan the QR code to learn more about projectile motion.

Things I have learned in this chapter:

- solving quadratic equations by factoring
- solving quadratic equations by graphing
- solving quadratic equations using the quadratic formula
- determining the nature of roots using the discriminant
- solving word problems involving quadratic equations

My Notes:

_____

_____

_____

_____

_____

_____

_____

_____

_____

_____

Chapter 4

Knowledge and Understanding

Circle the correct answers.

① What are the roots of $-2(x - 1)(x + 3) = 0$?

    A. 2 and 3   B. 1 and 3

    C. -2 and 3   D. 1 and -3

② Which equation has different x-intercepts from the other three?

    A. $y = x(x - 2)$ B. $y = -2x(2 + x)$

    C. $y = x^2 - 2x$ D. $y = 2x - x^2$

③ A quadratic relation has one x-intercept at $\dfrac{-4 - \sqrt{21}}{5}$. What is the other x-intercept?

    A. $\dfrac{-4 - \sqrt{-21}}{5}$ B. $\dfrac{4 + \sqrt{21}}{5}$

    C. $\dfrac{-4 - \sqrt{21}}{-5}$ D. $\dfrac{-4 + \sqrt{21}}{5}$

④ A quadratic equation has an axis of symmetry at $x = -3$ and one of its x-intercepts at 2. What is the other x-intercept?

    A. -8   B. -5

    C. -1   D. 7

⑤ Consider a quadratic relation in standard form. Which of the following cannot be determined using the a, b, and c values?

    A. x-intercept(s)   B. discriminant

    C. axis of symmetry   D. y-intercept

⑥ What is the discriminant of a perfect-square trinomial?

    A. $D = 0$ B. $D = 1$

    C. $D > 0$ D. $D < 0$

⑦ What is not a possible number of real roots for a quadratic equation?

    A. 0   B. 1

    C. 2   D. 3

⑧ Which statement best illustrates that the equation $2x^2 + 3x + 5 = 0$ has no real roots?

    A. $3^2 - 4(2)(5) < 0$ B. $2x^2 + 3x + 5$ cannot be factored.

    C. $2x^2 + 3x + 5 = 2(x + \dfrac{3}{4})^2 + \dfrac{31}{8}$ D. none of the above

Find the *x*-intercepts of each quadratic relation. Then match each equation with its graph.

⑨ **A** $y = (x + 1)(x + 3)$ **B** $y = (2x + 3)^2$ **C** $y = 2x^2 - 4x + 3$

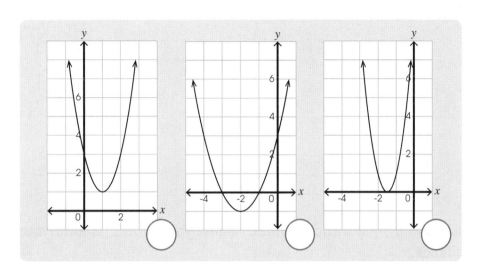

Use the given information to write the equation in the specified form.

⑩ with zeros at -3 and 5 and passes through (3,-2) in factored form

⑪ with zeros at -5 and 2 and an optimal value of -49 in standard form

Determine the number of roots by finding the discriminant of each quadratic equation.

⑫ $x^2 - 8x + 4 = 0$

⑬ $7x^2 + 2x + 10 = 0$

⑭ $-x^2 + 2x - 4 = 0$

⑮ $-3x^2 - 12x - 12 = 0$

Solve the equations by factoring. Show your work.

⑯ $x^2 - 5x - 24 = 0$

⑰ $3x^2 - 14x + 15 = 0$

⑱ $4x^2 + 11x + 6 = 0$

⑲ $6x^2 - 32x + 10 = 0$

Solve the equations by quadratic formula. Show your work. Round your answers to two decimal places.

⑳ $3x^2 - 5x + 2 = 0$

㉑ $4x^2 - 9x + 3 = 0$

㉒ $7x^2 - 17x - 40 = 0$

㉓ $-3x^2 - 2x + 5 = 0$

Determine whether each given value is a root for the equation.

㉔ $x = \frac{1}{3}$ and $3x^2 - 10x + 3 = 0$

㉕ $x = \frac{3}{4}$ and $4x^2 + 11x - 3 = 0$

Application

Answer the questions. Show your work.

㉖ The path of a soccer ball is given by $h = -0.1d^2 + 1.1d + 0.5$, where h is the height above the ground in metres and d is the horizontal distance travelled in metres.

  a. What was the horizontal distance travelled before it landed on the ground?

  b. What was the maximum height of the soccer ball?

㉗ Each customer at a sticker shop buys an average of 6 rolls of stickers at $4 per roll. Statistics show that for every $0.25 decrease in price, a customer will buy an additional roll.

  a. At what price will the revenue from the stickers be $28 per customer?

  b. What is the maximum revenue per customer?

㉘ A right triangle has two short sides that differ in length by 2 cm. The hypotenuse is 4 cm longer than the shortest side. What are the lengths of all three sides?

㉙ Two positive integers differ by 6. If the integers are squared and then added, the result is 146. What are the integers?

Communication

Answer the questions.

㉚ Explain how the discriminant is used to determine the number of roots a quadratic equation has.

㉛ For a quadratic equation in the form $ax^2 + bx + c = 0$, where a, b, and c are integers ($a \neq 0$), explain why this statement is always true: if $ac < 0$, then root(s) must exist.

㉜ Consider two quadratic equations $p(x - q)^2 + r = 0$ and $-p(x - q)^2 + r = 0$, where $p \neq 0$. Determine the number of roots for $-p(x - q)^2 + r = 0$ when $p(x - q)^2 + r = 0$ has 0, 1, or 2 real roots.

Thinking

Answer the questions. Show your work.

㉝ Determine the value of k if each equation has one real root.

a. $kx^2 - kx + 8 = 0$

b. $kx^2 + 5x + k = 0$

㉞ Determine the point(s) of intersection of the parabolas $y = 3x^2 - x + 8$ and $y = -x^2 + 4x + 7$, if there are any.

Final Test

Circle the correct answers.

① Which is not a perfect-square trinomial?

A. $x^2 - 4x + 4$ B. $x^3 + 8x^2$

C. $(2x - 3)^2$ D. $9x^2 + 30x + 25$

② Which does not represent a difference of squares?

A. $(x - 2)(x + 2)$ B. $(x + 5)(x - 5)$

C. $x^2 - 16$ D. $(x - 1)^2$

③ The graph of $y = x^2$ is reflected in the x-axis, translated 3 units right and 5 units up. What is the equation of the parabola?

A. $y = (x - 3)^2 + 5$ B. $y = -(x + 3)^2 + 5$

C. $y = -(x + 3)^2 - 5$ D. $y = -(x - 3)^2 + 5$

④ Which of the following equations has a root of -3?

A. $x^2 + 3x = 0$ B. $x^2 - 2x - 3 = 0$

C. $x^2 - x - 3 = 0$ D. none of the above

⑤ Which graph has the point with the smallest y-intercept?

A. $y = x^2 + 3$ B. $y = (x + 2)^2 - 5$

C. $y = (x - 3)^2 + 4$ D. $y = 6x^2$

⑥ A quadratic equation in the form $ax^2 + bx + c = 0$ has no real roots. Which of the following may its parabola have?

A. $a > 0$ and a vertex of (3,-2) B. $a > 0$ and a vertex of (-3,2)

C. $a < 0$ and a vertex of (3,0) D. $a < 0$ and a vertex of (-3,2)

⑦ If the equation $kx^2 + 6x + 1 = 0$ has one real root, what is the value of k?

A. 0 B. 6

C. 9 D. 14

⑧ Which of the following is a root of $2x^2 - x - 6 = 0$?

A. 2 B. -2

C. 1 D. no real roots

Fully factor each polynomial.

⑨ $x^2 + x - 12$ ⑩ $3x^2 + 12x + 12$ ⑪ $32x^2 - 72$

Find the equation that models each parabola. Write it in standard form.

⑫ a vertex of (-4,7) and a
    y-intercept of 6

⑬ zeros at 5 and -3, passes through
    (-5,4)

Determine a quadratic relation that models each parabola. Write it in the specified form.

⑭

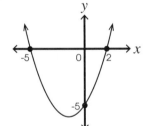

factored form: _____

⑮

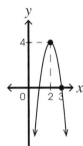

vertex form: _____

Convert each equation into vertex form. Then fill in the blanks.

⑯ $y = 2x^2 - 12x + 7$

⑰ $y = -3x^2 + 4x - 1$

vertex: _____

axis of symmetry: _____

direction of opening: _____

vertex: _____

axis of symmetry: _____

direction of opening: _____

Final Test

Find the zeros of each quadratic relation by factoring.

⑱ $y = 2x^2 - 4x - 70$

⑲ $y = 3x^2 + 11x - 4$

⑳ $y = 5(x - 2)^2 - 5$

Solve each equation using the quadratic formula. Round your answers to two decimal places.

㉑ $3x^2 + 8x - 3 = 0$

㉒ $x^2 = 6x + 2$

㉓ $8x^2 = -4x + 5$

Determine the discriminant of each quadratic equation. State the number of real roots each has.

㉔ $-4x^2 + 5x - 1 = 0$

㉕ $3x^2 - 12x + 12 = 0$

㉖ $\frac{1}{2}(x - 3)(x + 5) + 10 = 0$

State the transformations of the graph for each equation in relation to the graph of $y = x^2$. Then sketch it.

㉗ $y = 2(x + 3)^2 - 2$

㉘ $y = -2(x - 2)^2 - 1$

㉙ $y = -\dfrac{1}{4}(x - 1)^2 + 1$

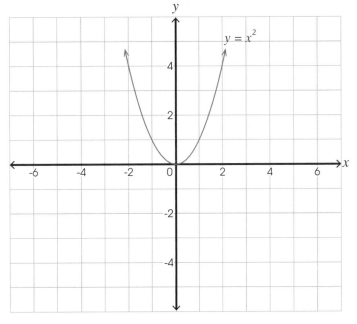

Application

Solve the problems. Show your work.

㉚ A circus performer jumped off a platform on a swing. The height of the performer from the ground, h, in metres, is modelled by $h = 0.6t^2 - 3.6t + 20$, where t is the time after he jumped in seconds. What was the minimum height of the performer from the ground? How many seconds after he jumped would he be at the minimum height?

㉛ A sky diver jumped out of an airplane 5.5 km above ground. The equation $H = 5500 - t^2$ is an approximation of the diver's altitude, H, in metres at t seconds after jumping out of the plane.

    a. How far had the diver fallen after 10 s?

    b. At an altitude of 1000 m, she opened the parachute. For how long was she in freefall from the plane?

③② The length of a rectangle is 4 cm more than triple its width. If its area is 20 cm², what are the dimensions of the rectangle?

③③ The sum of the squares of three positive consecutive odd integers is 1331. What are the three numbers?

③④ The local zoo would like to build a new rectangular enclosure using 320 m of fencing. Only three sides need to be built as one side of the enclosure will be against an existing building. What is the maximum area of the enclosure?

③⑤ The Yorkville Transit Commission has 140 000 riders daily, each paying $2. It is estimated that for every 10-cent increase in fare, 5000 riders will be lost. At what price will the maximum income be generated?

Answer the questions.

㊱ Explain how to tell if a relation is linear, quadratic, or neither using first and second differences.

㊲ Describe three different ways to solve a quadratic equation.

Thinking

Answer the questions. Show your work.

㊳ Determine the equation of the parabola, in standard form, that has the same shape and direction of opening as $y = 3x^2 - 18x + 29$ and has a vertex at (-5,-10).

㊴ The graph of $y = -2(x + 8)^2 - 4$ is translated such that its new graph has an axis of symmetry at $x = 1$ and passes through (-3,-14). Describe the translation.

Answers

Chapter 1: Operations with Polynomials

1.1 Factoring and Expanding Polynomials

1. $2 ; 2$
2. $3 ; 3$
3. $4 ; 4 ; 3$
4. $3 ; 3 ; x$
5. $2 ; 2 ; x^2 ; 5$
6. $5 ; 5 ; x^2 ; 2$
7. $3x ; 3x ; x ; 3$
8. $3x ; 3x ; x ; 2$
9. $x ; x ; 4x ; 1$
10. $2x ; 2x ; 3x ; 2$
11. $= 5(x + 3)$
12. $= 4(x - 3)$
13. $= 6(3x^2 + 1)$
14. $= 2(4x^2 + 2x + 1)$
15. $= 3x(xy + 2)$
16. $= xy(y + 2)$
17. $= (x + 5)(x + 2)$
18. $= (x - 3)(x - 4)$
19. $= (y + 1)(x + 2)$
20. $= (x + 2)(a + 1)$
21. $= (2y + 1)(x - 2)$
22. $= (2y + 1)(y - x)$
23. $= a(x + y) + 5(x + y)$
    $= (x + y)(a + 5)$
24. $= ax + ay + bx + by$
    $= a(x + y) + b(x + y)$
    $= (x + y)(a + b)$
25. $= x(a - b) + y(a - b)$
    $= (a - b)(x + y)$
26. $= y(x - 5) + 2(x - 5)$
    $= (x - 5)(y + 2)$
27. $= x(y + 2) + 3(y + 2)$
    $= (y + 2)(x + 3)$
28. $= 3x(x + 2) + 4(x + 2)$
    $= (x + 2)(3x + 4)$
29. $= x^2 + x + xy + y$
    $= x(x + 1) + y(x + 1)$
    $= (x + 1)(x + y)$
30. $= 5x^2 + 10x + 2xy + 4y$
    $= 5x(x + 2) + 2y(x + 2)$
    $= (x + 2)(5x + 2y)$
31. $= x^2 + x + 2x + 2$
    $= x^2 + 3x + 2$
32. $= x^2 - 3x + x - 3$
    $= x^2 - 2x - 3$
33. $= x^2 + 2x - 4x - 8$
    $= x^2 - 2x - 8$
34. $= x^2 + 2x + 5x + 10$
    $= x^2 + 7x + 10$
35. $= x^2 - 8x - x + 8$
    $= x^2 - 9x + 8$
36. $= x^2 + 5x - 5x - 25$
    $= x^2 - 25$
37. $= 2x^2 + 3x - 2x - 3$
    $= 2x^2 + x - 3$
38. $= 2x^2 + 2x + x + 1$
    $= 2x^2 + 3x + 1$
39. $= 3x^2 + 2x + 18x + 12$
    $= 3x^2 + 20x + 12$
40. $= 2x^2 - x - 12x + 6$
    $= 2x^2 - 13x + 6$
41. $= 4x^2 - 2x + 2x - 1$
    $= 4x^2 - 1$
42. $= x^2 + 2xy + xy + 2y^2$
    $= x^2 + 3xy + 2y^2$
43. $= x^3 + x^2y - xy - y^2$
44. correct
45. incorrect ; $3(2x^2 + 5x + 1)$
46. incorrect ; $6x^2y + 18xy^2 - 6xy$
47. incorrect ; $(x + 1)(2 - y)$
48. incorrect ; $-2x^2 - 5x + 2xy + 5y$
49. incorrect ; $x^3 + x^2y - 2xy - 2y^2$
50a. x b. 2 c. y d. $4mn$
   e. 1 f. ab
51a. x b. $3y$ c. $5x$ d. 2
   e. $4x - 2$ f. $5a - b + 3$
   g. $5x - y + 2$ h. $3m - n + 4$
52a. $x(x^2 + 5x - 1)$ b. $x(4x + y + 6)$
   c. $(y + 3)(12 - x)$ d. $(x - 5)(10 + x^2)$
   e. $2x(x^2 - 2x - 1)$ f. $xy(x - 2y + 3)$

53a. no   b. yes ; $2(x + 5)(x - 2)$
   c. no   d. yes ; $x^2(y + 1)^2$
   e. $2x(x - 3)^2$ f. no
54a. $x^2 - x - 12$ b. $x^2 - 3x - 10$
   c. $2x^2 + 13x + 15$ d. $2x^2 - 17x + 8$
   e. $xy + x + y^2 + y$ f. $x^3 + xy + 2x^2 + 2y$
55. Factoring a polynomial is the reverse of expanding a polynomial.
56. No, she is incorrect.
   (Suggested example) $(x + 1)(x - 1) = x^2 - 1$
57. $6(a + 2)$
58. Let x be an integer.
   $(x + 1)^2 - x^2$
   $= x^2 + 2x + 1 - x^2$
   $= 2x + 1$
   $2x$ is an even number and adding 1 to it must result in an odd number.
59. $4a + 1$ is an odd number. For the product to be divisible by 2, the other integer must be an even number.
60. $(3 + \sqrt{2})s^2$

1.2 Factorization

1. $5 ; 6 ; 5 ; 6$
   $x^2 - 6x + 5$; $(-5) + (-1) = -6$; $(-5) \times (-1) = 5$
   $x^2 - x - 20$; $4 + (-5) = -1$; $4 \times (-5) = -20$
   $x^2 + 3x - 18$; $(-3) + 6 = 3$; $(-3) \times 6 = -18$
2a. coefficient of the x term   b. constant
3. positive ; positive   4. negative ; positive
5. negative   6. $1 ; 1$ 7. $1 ; 8$
8. $2 ; 5$ 9. $1 ; 2$ 10. $3 ; 5$ 11. $1 ; 11$
12. $= (x + 1)(x + 3)$ 13. $= (x + 1)(x + 7)$
14. $= (x - 2)(x - 5)$ 15. $= (x - 1)(x - 3)$
16. $= (x + 5)(x - 9)$ 17. $= (x + 5)(x - 1)$
18. $= (x - 2)(x + 7)$ 19. $= (x - 4)(x - 6)$
20. $= (x - 2)(x - 4)$ 21. $= (x + 3)(x - 7)$
22. $= (x - 2)(x + 5)$ 23. $= (x + 1)(x - 8)$
24. $= (x + 2)(x + 8)$
25. no   26. no   27. $= (x - 1)(x + 4)$
28. $= (x - 2)(x - 5)$ 29. $= (x - 1)(x + 6)$
30. no   31. no   32. $= (x + 1)(x - 9)$
33. $x^2 ; 3x ; 2$ 34. $= 2(x^2 - 2x - 3)$
    $1 ; 2$ $= 2(x + 1)(x - 3)$
35. $= 4(x^2 + 5x + 7)$ 36. $= 4(x^2 - 5x + 6)$
                $= 4(x - 2)(x - 3)$
37. $= 2(x^2 + x + 2)$ 38. $= 3(2x^2 + x + 3)$
39. $= 2(x^2 + 2x - 3)$ 40. $= 2(x^2 - 2x - 3)$
    $= 2(x + 3)(x - 1)$ $= 2(x + 1)(x - 3)$
41. $= 2(3x^2 + 2x + 8)$ 42. $= x(x^2 - 4x - 5)$
                $= x(x - 5)(x + 1)$

Answers

43. $= y(x^2 - x - 20)$
    $= y(x - 5)(x + 4)$

44. $= 2x(x^2 + 5x - 6)$
    $= 2x(x - 1)(x + 6)$

45. $3 ; 2$
    $= 3x(x + 1) + 2(x + 1)$
    $= (x + 1)(3x + 2)$

46. $4 ; 9$
    $= 2x(3x+2)+3(3x+2)$
    $= (3x + 2)(2x + 3)$

47. $8 ; 1$
    $= 2x(x + 4) + (x + 4)$
    $= (x + 4)(2x + 1)$

48. $= 6x^2 + 3x + 4x + 2$
    $= 3x(2x+1)+2(2x+1)$
    $= (2x + 1)(3x + 2)$

49. $= 4x^2 + 12x - x - 3$
    $= 4x(x + 3) - (x + 3)$
    $= (x + 3)(4x - 1)$

50. $= 10x^2 - 15x - 4x + 6$
    $= 5x(2x-3)-2(2x-3)$
    $= (2x - 3)(5x - 2)$

51. $= 8x^2 - 4x + 2x - 1$
    $= 4x(2x - 1) + (2x - 1)$
    $= (2x - 1)(4x + 1)$

52. $= 2x^2 + 8x - x - 4$
    $= 2x(x + 4) - (x + 4)$
    $= (x + 4)(2x - 1)$

53. $= 3x^2 - 6x - x + 2$
    $= 3x(x - 2) - (x - 2)$
    $= (x - 2)(3x - 1)$

54. $= 3x^2 - 3x - 5x + 5$
    $= 3x(x - 1) - 5(x - 1)$
    $= (x - 1)(3x - 5)$

55. $= 4x^2 - 4x - x + 1$
    $= 4x(x - 1) - (x - 1)$
    $= (x - 1)(4x - 1)$

56. $= 2x^2 - 8x - x + 4$
    $= 2x(x - 4) - (x - 4)$
    $= (x - 4)(2x - 1)$

57. $2 ; 1$
    $3 ; 2$
    $2 ; 1 ; 3 ; 2$

58. $2 ; 3$
    $1 ; -1$
    $2x + 3 ; x - 1$

59. $4 ; 1$
    $2 ; -1$
    $4x + 1 ; 2x - 1$

60. $3 ; 2$
    $1 ; 1$
    $= (3x + 2)(x + 1)$

61. $2 ; -3$
    $1 ; -2$
    $= (2x - 3)(x - 2)$

62. $= (2x + 3)(x + 3)$

63. $= (x + 1)(3x + 4)$

64. not factorable

65. $= (x - 1)(2x - 5)$

66. $= (x + 1)(4x - 5)$

67. not factorable

68. $= (5x - 2)(x - 2)$

69a. $(x + 2)(x - 1)$
   b. $(x + 3)(x - 1)$
   c. $(x - 2)(x + 1)$
   d. $(x + 4)(x - 1)$
   e. $(x + 2)(x + 5)$
   f. $2(x - 3)(x - 5)$
   g. $3(x - 3)(x + 1)$
   h. $2(x - 5)(x + 3)$
   i. $3(x - 4)(x - 2)$

70a. not factorable
   b. factorable
   c. not factorable
   d. factorable
   e. factorable
   f. not factorable

71a. $(5x - 2)(x - 1)$
   b. $3(x - 1)(x - 6)$
   c. $(2x + 3)(x + 8)$
   d. $(2x - 1)(3x + 2)$
   e. $2(4x - 3)(x + 2)$
   f. $2(x + 7)(x - 5)$
   g. $4x(x + 5)(x + 1)$
   h. $2(5x - 2)(x + 3)$
   i. $3(2x + 1)(3x - 4)$

72a. not factorable
   b. factorable
   c. factorable
   d. not factorable
   e. factorable
   f. not factorable

73a. $(x - 9)$ b. $(x + 6)$ c. $(x + 4)$
   d. $(3x - 1)$ e. $(x - 3)$ f. $3(x - 2)$

74. No, she is incorrect. (Suggested example)
    $x^2 - 4 = (x - 2)(x + 2)$
    The binomial $x^2 - 4$ is factored into two binomials.

75. To determine whether a trinomial can be factored, identify the values of a, b, and c. Then determine whether there are any integers p, q, r, and s, such that $pq = a$, $rs = c$, and $ps + rq = b$. If there exists such a set of integers, then the trinomial can be factored.

76a. 6 or 9   b. 5 or 7   c. 4 or 10

77a. yes   b. no   c. yes

78a. not factorable   b. $(4m - 3n)(m + n)$
   c. $2(x + y)(x + y + 3)$

1.3 Perfect-square Trinomials and Differences of Squares

1a. $x ; 3$
    $x ; 3$
   b. $x ; 4$
    $x ; 4$
   c. $x^2 ; x ; 81 ; 9$
    $x ; 9$
   d. $x^2 ; x ; 25 ; 5$
    $x ; 5$

2a. $x ; 2$
    $x ; 2 ; x ; 2$
   b. $x ; 5$
    $x ; 5 ; x ; 5$
   c. $x^2 ; x ; 100 ; 10$
    $x ; 10 ; x ; 10$
   d. $x^2 ; x ; 16 ; 4$
    $x ; 4 ; x ; 4$

3. $= (x + 6)^2$ 4. $= (x + 5)^2$ 5. $= (x - 8)^2$
6. $= (x - 1)^2$ 7. $= (3x + 1)^2$ 8. $= (2x + 3)^2$
9. $= (2x - 1)^2$ 10. $= (3x + 2)^2$ 11. $= (5x - 1)^2$
12. $= (3x - 1)^2$ 13. $= (4x + 1)^2$ 14. $= (5x + 2)^2$
15. $= (x + 9)^2$ 16. $= (x - 6)^2$ 17. $= (2x + 5)^2$
18. $= (3x - 2)^2$

19. not a perfect-square trinomial

20. $= (5x - 9)^2$ 21. $= (5x - 2)^2$

22. not a perfect-square trinomial

23. $= (x + 1)(x - 1)$ 24. $= (x + 12)(x - 12)$
25. $= (x + 11)(x - 11)$ 26. $= (x + 6)(x - 6)$
27. $= (5x + 4)(5x - 4)$ 28. $= (2x + 3)(2x - 3)$
29. $= (2x + 5)(2x - 5)$ 30. $= 9(x^2 - 4)$
                              $= 9(x + 2)(x - 2)$

31. $= 4(16x^2 - 25)$ 32. $= 20(x^2 - 4)$
    $= 4(4x + 5)(4x - 5)$ $= 20(x + 2)(x - 2)$

33. $= 3(x^2 - 10x + 25)$ 34. $= -2(x^2 - 14x + 49)$
    $= 3(x - 5)^2$ $= -2(x - 7)^2$

35. $= 4(x^2 - 25)$ 36. $= 4(x^2 - 12x + 36)$
    $= 4(x + 5)(x - 5)$ $= 4(x - 6)^2$

37. Sum of the areas: $4a^2 + 4ab + b^2 = (2a + b)^2$
    Side length: $\sqrt{4a^2 + 4ab + b^2} = \sqrt{(2a + b)^2} = 2a+b$
    The expression for the area is $4a^2 + 4ab + b^2$
    and the side length is $2a + b$.

38. $(2x + 5)^2 - (x - 2)^2$
    $= 4x^2 + 20x + 25 - x^2 + 4x - 4$
    $= 3x^2 + 24x + 21$
    $= 3(x^2 + 8x + 7)$
    $= 3(x + 7)(x + 1)$

39a. $(x + 2)^2$ b. $(x + 4)^2$ c. $(5x + 1)^2$ d. $(x - 5)^2$
    e. not a perfect-square trinomial
    f. not a perfect-square trinomial
    g. $(2x - 5)^2$ h. not a perfect-square trinomial
    i. $(3x - 5)^2$

40a. not a difference of squares
    b. $(x + 6)(x - 6)$
    c. not a difference of squares
    d. $(2x + 7)(2x - 7)$
    e. not a difference of squares
    f. not a difference of squares
    g. $(5x + 1)(5x - 1)$ h. $(2x + y)(2x - y)$
    i. $(3x + 4y)(3x - 4y)$

41a. $x^2 - 6x + 9$ b. $x^2 - 49$
    $= x^2 - 3x - 3x + 9$ $= x^2 + 7x - 7x - 49$
    $= x(x - 3) - 3(x - 3)$ $= x(x + 7) - 7(x + 7)$
    $= (x - 3)(x - 3)$ $= (x + 7)(x - 7)$
    $= (x - 3)^2$

    c. $4x^2 + 4x + 1$ d. $9x^2 - 4$
    $= 4x^2 + 2x + 2x + 1$ $= 9x^2 + 6x - 6x - 4$
    $= 2x(2x + 1) + (2x + 1)$ $= 3x(3x+2) - 2(3x+2)$
    $= (2x + 1)(2x + 1)$ $= (3x + 2)(3x - 2)$
    $= (2x + 1)^2$

42a. $4(x - 5)^2$ b. $25(x + 2)(x - 2)$
    c. $(9x + 5)(9x - 5)$ d. $(3x - 7)^2$
    e. $16(2x^2 + 3)(2x^2 - 3)$ f. $2(3x^2 - 5)^2$

43a. $4(a - 5)$ b. $2m(m + n)$
    c. $(3x^2 + 5y)$ d. $2(4a + b)$

44. (Suggested answers)
    a. 4   b. $4x$ or $-4x$ c. $48x$ or $-48x$

45a. 1   b. 3   c. 1

46. $29^2 - 19^2 = (29 + 19)(29 - 19) = 48 \times 10 = 480$

47. Yes, he is correct.
    Original polynomial:
      $25 + 4x^2 + 20x$
    $= 4x^2 + 20x + 25$
    $= (2x + 5)^2$ ← a perfect-square trinomial
    A multiple of 3 of the polynomial:
      $60x + 75 + 12x^2$
    $= 12x^2 + 60x + 75$
    $= 3(2x + 5)^2$ ← a perfect-square trinomial
    So, a multiple of the perfect-square
    trinomial is also a perfect-square trinomial.

48a. $(3a + 2b)^2 - 9a^2 - 4b^2$
    $= 9a^2 + 12ab + 4b^2 - 9a^2 - 4b^2$
    $= 12ab$
    The area is $12ab$.
    b. $4(3a + 2b) = 12a + 8b$
    The perimeter is $12a + 8b$.

1.4 Completing the Square

1. 10 ; 25   2. -8 ; 16   3. 2 ; 1   4. 8 ; 16
   25 ; 5   16 ; 4   1 ; 1   16 ; 4

5. 4 ; 2   6. 49 ; 7   7. $6x$; 9   8. 25 ; 5
                                x ; 3

9. 4 ; 9   10. 5 ; $2x$; 1   11. 1 ; 1
   4 ; 3   5 ; 1

12. 4 ; $(x - 2)^2$ 13. 25 ; $(x - 5)^2$
14. 9 ; $(x + 3)^2$ 15. 6.25 ; $(x - 2.5)^2$
16. 0.25 ; $(x + 0.5)^2$ 17. $x^2 - 2x + 1$; $2(x - 1)^2$
18. $\dfrac{9}{4}$; $\dfrac{3}{2}$ 19. 9 ; 9 ; 9 ; 9 ; 3 ; 8

20. $= (x^2 + 4x + 4 - 4) + 2$ 21. $= (x^2 - 6x + 9 - 9) - 2$
    $= (x^2 + 4x + 4) - 4 + 2$ $= (x^2 - 6x + 9) - 9 - 2$
    $= (x + 2)^2 - 2$ $= (x - 3)^2 - 11$

22. $= (x^2 - 10x + 25 - 25) + 3$
    $= (x^2 - 10x + 25) - 25 + 3$
    $= (x - 5)^2 - 22$

23. $= (x^2 + 7x + 12.25 - 12.25) + 1$
    $= (x^2 + 7x + 12.25) - 12.25 + 1$
    $= (x + 3.5)^2 - 11.25$

24. $= (x^2 - 3x + 2.25 - 2.25) - 5$
    $= (x^2 - 3x + 2.25) - 2.25 - 5$
    $= (x - 1.5)^2 - 7.25$

25. 16 ; 16 ; 16 ; 32 ; 4 ; 31

26. $= 3(x^2 + 4x) - 2$
    $= 3(x^2 + 4x + 4 - 4) - 2$
    $= 3(x^2 + 4x + 4) - 12 - 2$
    $= 3(x + 2)^2 - 14$

27. $= 2(x^2 - 2x) + 1$ 28. $= 4(x^2 + 2x) + 5$
    $= 2(x^2 - 2x + 1 - 1) + 1$ $= 4(x^2 + 2x + 1 - 1) + 5$
    $= 2(x^2 - 2x + 1) - 2 + 1$ $= 4(x^2 + 2x + 1) - 4 + 5$
    $= 2(x - 1)^2 - 1$ $= 4(x + 1)^2 + 1$

29. $= 3(x^2 + 3x) + 4$
    $= 3(x^2 + 3x + 2.25 - 2.25) + 4$
    $= 3(x^2 + 3x + 2.25) - 6.75 + 4$
    $= 3(x + 1.5)^2 - 2.75$

30. $= 2(x^2 - 3x) - 5$
    $= 2(x^2 - 3x + 2.25 - 2.25) - 5$
    $= 2(x^2 - 3x + 2.25) - 4.5 - 5$
    $= 2(x - 1.5)^2 - 9.5$

Answers

31. $= 3(x^2 + 5x) - 2$
    $= 3(x^2 + 5x + 6.25 - 6.25) - 2$
    $= 3(x^2 + 5x + 6.25) - 18.75 - 2$
    $= 3(x + 2.5)^2 - 20.75$

32. $= x^2 + 8x + 15$
    $= (x^2 + 8x + 16 - 16) + 15$
    $= (x^2 + 8x + 16) - 16 + 15$
    $= (x + 4)^2 - 1$

33. $= x^2 + 4x - 21$ 34. $= x^2 - 2x - 24$
    $= (x^2 + 4x + 4 - 4) - 21$ $= (x^2 - 2x + 1 - 1) - 24$
    $= (x^2 + 4x + 4) - 4 - 21$ $= (x^2 - 2x + 1) - 1 - 24$
    $= (x + 2)^2 - 25$ $= (x - 1)^2 - 25$

35. $= 4x^2 + 16x + 15$
    $= 4(x^2 + 4x) + 15$
    $= 4(x^2 + 4x + 4 - 4) + 15$
    $= 4(x^2 + 4x + 4) - 16 + 15$
    $= 4(x + 2)^2 - 1$

36. $= 4x^2 - 12x + 5$
    $= 4(x^2 - 3x) + 5$
    $= 4(x^2 - 3x + 2.25 - 2.25) + 5$
    $= 4(x^2 - 3x + 2.25) - 9 + 5$
    $= 4(x - 1.5)^2 - 4$

37. $= 4x^2 - 4x - 15$
    $= 4(x^2 - x) - 15$
    $= 4(x^2 - x + 0.25 - 0.25) - 15$
    $= 4(x^2 - x + 0.25) - 1 - 15$
    $= 4(x - 0.5)^2 - 16$

38a. 36   b. 4   c. 100   d. 169
    e. 36   f. 5   g. 25   h. 20.25

39a. $(x + 5)^2 - 25$ b. $(x - 7)^2 - 49$
    c. $(x - 6)^2 - 31$ d. $(x + 3)^2 + 2$
    e. $(x + 0.5)^2 + 2.75$ f. $(x + 1.5)^2 - 3.25$
    g. $2(x - 4)^2 - 32$ h. $2(x + 2)^2 - 8$
    i. $2(x - 6)^2 - 71$ j. $3(x + 8)^2 - 204$
    k. $3(x + 1.5)^2 - 6.75$ l. $5(x - 2.5)^2 - 21.25$

40a. $(x + 1)^2 - 1$ b. $(x - 4)^2 - 15$
    c. $2(x - 1.5)^2 - 4.5$ d. $3(x + \frac{2}{3})^2 - \frac{28}{3}$
    e. $2(x + 0.75)^2 - 6.125$ f. $(x + 1)^2 - 1$
    g. $(x - 3)^2 - 25$ h. $4(x + 1)^2 - 9$
    i. $(x - 1.5)^2 - 0.25$ j. $2(x - 1.75)^2 - 1.125$

41. Yes, completing the square can be applied to all polynomials in the form $ax^2 + bx + c$.

42. It is incorrect because the x term contains a coefficient of 2. The x term must have a coefficient of 1 after completing the square.

43. In Simon's solution, he neglected to subtract 4 when creating the perfect-square trinomial. In Rex's solution, he neglected to multiply -4 by 3 when bringing it outside the brackets.

Quiz 1

1. B   2. D   3. A   4. C
5. D   6. D   7. B   8. C
9. $= x^2 + 5x$ 10. $= 6x^2 - 3xy$
11. $= 30x^2 + 10x - 6x - 2$ 12. $= 3(x^2 + 2x + 1)$
    $= 30x^2 + 4x - 2$ $= 3x^2 + 6x + 3$
13. $= 4a^2 - 4ab + b^2$ 14. $= 2x^2 + 6xy - xy - 3y^2$
                                   $= 2x^2 + 5xy - 3y^2$
15. $= 3x(x + 1)$ 16. $= 2x(4x - 1)$
17. fully factored   18. fully factored
19. $= 2xy(x + 3)$ 20. $= 2x^2(x^2 - 2x + 1)$
                                   $= 2x^2(x - 1)^2$

21. $x^2 + bx + c$ •   • $(x - r)(x - s)$
    $x^2 - bx + c$ •   • $(x + r)(x - s)$
    $x^2 + bx - c$ •   • $(x + r)(x + s)$
    $x^2 - bx - c$ •   • $(x - r)(x + s)$

22. $= x^2 + 2x + 1$ 23. $= x^2 - 14x + 49$
    $= (x + 1)^2$ $= (x - 7)^2$
24. $= x^2 + 16x + 64$ 25. $= 4x^2 - 20x + 25$
    $= (x + 8)^2$ $= (2x - 5)^2$
26. $= 4x^2 + 36x + 81$ 27. $= 9x^2 - 27x + 20.25$
    $= (2x + 9)^2$ $= (3x - 4.5)^2$
28. $= (x^2 - 2x + 1 - 1) - 1$ 29. $= (2x - 5)^2$
    $= (x - 1)^2 - 2$
30. $= (x^2 - 5x + 6.25 - 6.25) - 15$
    $= (x^2 - 5x + 6.25) - 6.25 - 15$
    $= (x - 2.5)^2 - 21.25$
31. $= 3x(y - 2) + y(y - 2)$ 32. $= (x^2 + 6x + 9 - 9) + 1$
    $= (y - 2)(3x + y)$ $= (x^2 + 6x + 9) - 9 + 1$
                                   $= (x + 3)^2 - 8$
33. $= (4x - y)^2$
34. $= -3(x^2 + 10x) - 68$
    $= -3(x^2 + 10x + 25 - 25) - 68$
    $= -3(x^2 + 10x + 25) + 75 - 68$
    $= -3(x + 5)^2 + 7$
35. $= 2(16x^2 - 81)$ 36. $= 4(x^2 - 7x + 10)$
    $= 2(4x + 9)(4x - 9)$ $= 4(x - 2)(x - 5)$
37. $= (x^2 - 8x) - 12$
    $= (x^2 - 8x + 16 - 16) - 12$
    $= (x^2 - 8x + 16) - 16 - 12$
    $= (x - 4)^2 - 28$
38. $= (x - 5)(x - 7)$
39. $= 2(x^2 + 2.5x) + 12$
    $= 2(x^2 + 2.5x + 1.5625 - 1.5625) + 12$
    $= 2(x^2 + 2.5x + 1.5625) - 3.125 + 12$
    $= 2(x + 1.25)^2 + 8.875$
40. $= 4x^2 + 20x + 25$
    $= 4(x^2 + 5x) + 25$
    $= 4(x^2 + 5x + 6.25 - 6.25) + 25$
    $= 4(x^2 + 5x + 6.25) - 25 + 25$
    $= 4(x + 2.5)^2$

41. $= 9x^2 + 9x - 10$
$= 9(x^2 + x) - 10$
$= 9(x^2 + x + 0.25 - 0.25) - 10$
$= 9(x + 0.5)^2 - 12.25$

42. $= -2x^2 + 12x - 11$
$= -2(x^2 - 6x) - 11$
$= -2(x^2 - 6x + 9 - 9) - 11$
$= -2(x - 3)^2 + 7$

43. $x - 8$ 44. $x + 9$ 45. $3(x + 3)$ 46. $5x - 1$

47. cannot be factored ; no

48. $= -6(x - 1)^2$; yes   49. $= 2(x^2 - 2x + 3)$; no

50. $12x^2 + 9x - 3$
$= 3(4x^2 + 3x - 1)$
$= 3(4x - 1)(x + 1)$ ⇒ Width: $3(x + 1)$
Perimeter: $2(4x - 1) + 2(3(x + 1))$
$= 8x - 2 + 6x + 6$
$= 14x + 4$
The width is $3(x + 1)$ and the perimeter is $14x + 4$.

51. $(5x + (3x + 4))h \div 2 = 8x^2 - 2$
$(4x + 2)h = 8x^2 - 2$
$2(2x + 1)h = 2(4x^2 - 1)$
$2(2x + 1)h = 2(2x + 1)(2x - 1)$
$h = 2x - 1$
The height of the trapezoid is $2x - 1$.

52. Area: $4a^2 + 24ab + xb^2$ ← a perfect-square trinomial
$2(\sqrt{4a^2})(\sqrt{xb^2}) = 24ab$
$2(2a)(b\sqrt{x}) = 24ab$
$\sqrt{x} = 6$
$x = 36$
$4a^2 + 24ab + 36b^2 = (2a + 6b)^2$
She needs 36 squares of b^2.

53. Area: $a^2 + 12ab + xb^2$ ← a perfect-square trinomial
$2(\sqrt{a^2})(\sqrt{xb^2}) = 12ab$
$2(a)(b\sqrt{x}) = 12ab$
$\sqrt{x} = 6$
$x = 36$
$a^2 + 12ab + 36b^2 = (a + 6b)^2$
$50 - 36 = 14$
The largest square has an area of $a^2 + 12ab + 36b^2$, and 14 pieces of b^2 squares are left over.

54. No. A perfect-square trinomial multiplied by a perfect square will result in a perfect-square trinomial. (Suggested example)
$x^2 + 2x + 1 = (x + 1)^2$
$4(x^2 + 2x + 1) = (2x + 2)^2$
Both $x^2 + 2x + 1$ and $4(x^2 + 2x + 1)$ are perfect-square trinomials.

55. To determine c, divide b by 2 and square it.

56. (Suggested examples)
1 unique factor: $x^2 + 2x + 1 = (x + 1)^2$
2 unique factors: $x^2 + 3x + 2 = (x + 1)(x + 2)$
3 unique factors: $2x^2 + 6x + 4 = 2(x + 1)(x + 2)$

57. It is not the correct form because the coefficient of the x term of the given expression is not 1. To convert the expression into the correct form, factor out the coefficient of the x term.
$(2x + 10)^2 - 1$
$= (2(x + 5))^2 - 1$
$= 2^2(x + 5)^2 - 1$
$= 4(x + 5)^2 - 1$

58. Let x be the first integer.
$x^2 + (x + 1)^2 + (x + 2)^2 + (x + 3)^2$
$= x^2 + x^2 + 2x + 1 + x^2 + 4x + 4 + x^2 + 6x + 9$
$= 4x^2 + 12x + 14$
$= 2(2x^2 + 6x + 7)$
Since 2 is a factor of the final sum, the sum is divisible by 2, so it is an even number.

59a. $ax^2 - 2ax - 3a$ b. $ax^2 - 2ax - 3a$
$= a(x^2 - 2x - 3)$ $= a(x^2 - 2x) - 3a$
$= a(x - 3)(x + 1)$ $= a(x^2 - 2x + 1 - 1) - 3a$
                               $= a(x - 1)^2 - 4a$

Chapter 2: Forms of Quadratic Relations

2.1 Parabolas

1a. 4   b. -2   c. downward
2a. 1   b. 1   c. upward
 3. -2 and 2 ; 1   4. 0 and 4 ; 0
 5. A graph has no x-intercepts if it does not cross the x-axis. The parabola either opens upward above the x-axis or opens downward below the x-axis.
 6. It must be 0.
 7. A: -3 and -1 ; 3 ; $x = -2$; (-2,-1) ; upward
    B: none ; -1 ; $x = 0$; (0,-1) ; downward
    C: 2 ; 4 ; $x = 2$; (2,0) ; upward
 8. 4 ; maximum   9. -2 ; minimum
10. 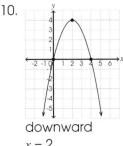   11.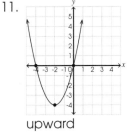

downward   upward
$x = 2$ $x = -2$
4   -4
maximum   minimum
0   0

Answers

12. y: -1 ; 0 ; 3
    1st diff.: -1 ; 1 ; 3
    2nd diff.: 2 ; 2 ; 2

13. y: 0 ; 3 ; 4 ; 3 ; 0
    1st diff.: 3 ; 1 ; -1 ; -3
    2nd diff.: -2 ; -2 ; -2

14.

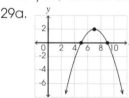

15a. positive ; upward
   b. negative; downward
16. T
17. F
18. T
19. F
20. T

21. A: upward ; 1   B: upward ; -1
    C: downward ; 1   D: downward ; -1
    B ; C ; D ; A

22. 2 ; 1 ; -1

23. $x = -\dfrac{1}{2(-2)} = \dfrac{1}{4}$

24. $x = -\dfrac{3}{2(\frac{1}{2})} = -3$

25. $x = -\dfrac{-6}{2(-\frac{1}{4})} = -12$

26. For a quadratic relation in standard form $(ax^2 + bx + c)$, the x-coordinate of the vertex is $-\dfrac{b}{2a}$. The y-coordinate can be found by substituting the x-coordinate into the quadratic relation. The vertex of $y = 2x^2 + 4x - 1$ is (-1,-3).

27a. $x = 1$; (1,-1) ; 0 and 2 ; 0
   b. $x = 2$; (2,0) ; 2 ; 4
   c. $x = -2$; (-2,-1) ; none ; -3
   d. $x = 1$; (1,4) ; -1 and 3 ; 3

28a. yes ; upward   b. no
   c. yes ; downward

29a.   b.

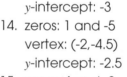

30a. It is a minimum.
   b. It is a negative number.
31a. The parabola touches the x-axis at one point and does not cross it.
   b. The vertex is (6,0).
   c. The optimal value is a maximum because the graph opens downward.
32a. upward ; -1 ; $x = -1$ b. downward; 2; $x = -2$
   c. downward ; -1 ; $x = 6$ d. upward ; 7 ; $x = 0$

2.2 Factored Form

1. A: 3   B: -3   C: 2
   D: -2   E: -2 ; 3   F: 2 ; 3
   C ; D ; A
   B ; F ; E

2. 1 ; 5 ; 3

3. $x = \dfrac{1 + (-3)}{2} = -1$

4. $x = \dfrac{4 + (-1)}{2} = \dfrac{3}{2}$

5. $x = \dfrac{0 + (-3)}{2} = -\dfrac{3}{2}$

6. $x = \dfrac{3 + (-2)}{2} = \dfrac{1}{2}$

7. 4 ; -6 ; -1 ; -1 ; -50 ; -48

8. -1 ; 3 ; $x = 1$; (1,-2) ; $-\dfrac{3}{2}$

9. 2, 6 ; $x = 4$; (4,4) ; -12

10. -1, -3 ; $x = -2$; (-2,3) ; -9

11. $y = (x + 3)(x + 1)$
    • zeros: -3 and -1
    • vertex: $x = \dfrac{-3 + (-1)}{2} = -2$
      $y = (-2 + 3)(-2 + 1) = -1$
      (-2,-1)
    • y-intercept: $y = (0 + 3)(0 + 1) = 3$

    $y = x(x - 2)$
    • zeros: 0 and 2
    • vertex: $x = \dfrac{0 + 2}{2} = 1$
      $y = (1)(1 - 2) = -1$
      (1,-1)
    • y-intercept: $y = (0)(0 - 2) = 0$

    $y = 2(x - 2)^2$
    • zero: 2
    • vertex: $x = 2$
      $y = 2(2 - 2)^2 = 0$
      (2,0)
    • y-intercept: $y = 2(0 - 2)^2 = 8$

12. 0 and -4 ; (-2,4) ; 0
13. zeros: -3 and 3
    vertex: (0,-3)
    y-intercept: -3
14. zeros: 1 and -5
    vertex: (-2,-4.5)
    y-intercept: -2.5
15. zeros: 4 and -2
    vertex: (1,2.25)
    y-intercept: 2

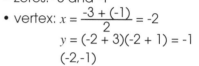

16. $y = a(x - 2)(x - 6)$
    $2 = a(4 - 2)(4 - 6)$
    $2 = -4a$
    $a = -\dfrac{1}{2}$
    $y = -\dfrac{1}{2}(x - 2)(x - 6)$

17. $y = a(x - (-2))(x - (-5))$
    $y = a(x + 2)(x + 5)$
    $-4 = a(-4 + 2)(-4 + 5)$
    $-4 = -2a$
    $a = 2$
    $y = 2(x + 2)(x + 5)$

18. $y = a(x - 1)(x - (-2))$
    $y = a(x - 1)(x + 2)$
    $2 = a(0 - 1)(0 + 2)$
    $2 = -2a$
    $a = -1$
    $y = -(x - 1)(x + 2)$

19. $y = a(x - 0)(x - (-4))$
    $y = ax(x + 4)$
    $-1 = a(-2)(-2 + 4)$
    $-1 = -4a$
    $a = \dfrac{1}{4}$
    $y = \dfrac{1}{4}x(x + 4)$

20. $y = a(x - 5)(x - (-1))$
$y = a(x - 5)(x + 1)$
$10 = a(4 - 5)(4 + 1)$
$a = -2$
$y = -2(x - 5)(x + 1)$

21. $y = a(x - 4)(x - (-8))$
$y = a(x - 4)(x + 8)$
$-4 = a(-2 - 4)(-2 + 8)$
$a = \frac{1}{9}$
$y = \frac{1}{9}(x - 4)(x + 8)$

22. $y = a(x - (-6))^2$
$y = a(x + 6)^2$
$9 = a(0 + 6)^2$
$a = \frac{1}{4}$
$y = \frac{1}{4}(x + 6)^2$

23. $y = -(x^2 + x - 8x - 8)$
$y = -x^2 + 7x + 8$
8 and -1 ; 8

24. $y = 4x^2 - 12x$
0 and 3 ; 0

25. $y = -5(x^2 + 18x + 81)$
$y = -5x^2 - 90x - 405$
-9 ; -405

26. $y = \frac{1}{2}(x^2 + 2x + 3x + 6)$
$y = \frac{1}{2}x^2 + \frac{5}{2}x + 3$
-3 and -2 ; 3

27. $y = -\frac{3}{4}(x^2 + 6x - 2x - 12)$
$y = -\frac{3}{4}x^2 - 3x + 9$
2 and -6 ; 9

28. $y = a(x - 4)(x - (-2))$
$y = a(x - 4)(x + 2)$
$-27 = a(1 - 4)(1 + 2)$
$a = 3$
$y = 3(x - 4)(x + 2)$
$y = 3(x^2 + 2x - 4x - 8)$
$y = 3x^2 - 6x - 24$

29. $y = a(x - 0)(x - 8)$
$y = ax(x - 8)$
$8 = a(4)(4 - 8)$
$a = -\frac{1}{2}$
$y = -\frac{1}{2}x(x - 8)$
$y = -\frac{1}{2}x^2 + 4x$

30. $y = a(x - 6)^2$
$6 = a(0 - 6)^2$
$a = \frac{1}{6}$
$y = \frac{1}{6}(x - 6)^2$
$y = \frac{1}{6}(x^2 - 12x + 36)$
$y = \frac{1}{6}x^2 - 2x + 6$

31a.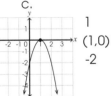
4 and -2
(1,-9)
-8

b.
2 and -2
(0,-2)
-2

c.
1
(1,0)
-2

d.
1 and -3
(-1,-6)
-4.5

32a. $y = x^2 - 5x - 14$; -2 and 7 ; y-intercept = -14
b. $y = -2x^2 - 12x + 54$; 3 and -9 ; y-intercept = 54
c. $y = \frac{1}{2}x^2 - 6x + 18$; 6 ; y-intercept = 18
d. $y = -x^2 + 100x$; 0 and 100 ; y-intercept = 0

33a. $y = -(x + 1)(x - 3)$; $y = -x^2 + 2x + 3$
b. $y = \frac{1}{4}(x - 1)(x - 5)$; $y = \frac{1}{4}x^2 - \frac{3}{2}x + \frac{5}{4}$
c. $y = -\frac{1}{3}(x + 3)^2$; $y = -\frac{1}{3}x^2 - 2x - 3$

34a. $y = -3x^2 - 12x + 15$
b. $y = -2x^2 - 8x - 6$
c. $y = \frac{1}{12}x^2 + x$
d. $y = -\frac{1}{3}x^2 - 2x$

35. (Suggested answers)
$y = (x - 7)(x + 3)$
$y = 2(x - 7)(x + 3)$
$y = -(x - 7)(x + 3)$

36a.
b. $y = -\frac{1}{9}(x - 6)(x + 6)$
c. It is 3 m high.

2.3 Vertex Form

1. A: a. 1   B: a. 1   C: a. -1 ; -1
   b. 1 ; 2   b. 1 ; -1   b. $(0 + 1)^2 - 1$; 0
   D: a. -1 ; -1
   b. $-\frac{1}{2}(0 + 1)^2 - 1$; $-1\frac{1}{2}$
   B ; C
   A ; D

2a. (3,-5)   b. 4   c. upward
3a. (-3,0)   b. -3   c. downward
4a. (-2,-1)   b. 1   c. upward
5a. (2,0)   b. -1   c. downward
6a. $y = \frac{1}{2}(x + 2)^2 - 1$ b. $y = (x - 3)^2 - 5$
c. $y = -\frac{1}{3}(x + 3)^2$ d. $y = -\frac{1}{4}(x - 2)^2$

7. (2,1) ; 5 ; upward ; $x = 2$; 1 ; min.
(-3,-2) ; -11 ; downward ; $x = -3$; -2 ; max.
(5,10) ; -65 ; downward ; $x = 5$; 10 ; max.
(-6,0) ; 9 ; upward ; $x = -6$; 0 ; min.

8-10.
$y = 2(x + 2)^2 - 3$
$y = \frac{1}{2}(x - 3)^2 - 2$
$y = -(x - 3)^2 + 6$

9. vertex: (-2,-3)
y-intercept: 5
opens upward

10. vertex: (3,-2)
y-intercept: 2.5
opens upward

11. 5 ; 2 ; 1 ; 3
$5 = a + 3$
$a = 2$
$2(x - 1)^2 + 3$

12. $-10 = a(5 - 1)^2 - 2$
$a = -\frac{1}{2}$
$y = -\frac{1}{2}(x - 1)^2 - 2$

13. $-1 = a(0 - 1)^2 + 2$
$-1 = a + 2$
$a = -3$
$y = -3(x - 1)^2 + 2$

14. $0 = a(1 - (-2))^2 + 9$
$0 = 9a + 9$
$a = -1$
$y = -(x + 2)^2 + 9$

15. $3 = a(0 - 1)^2 + 1$
$a = 2$
$y = 2(x - 1)^2 + 1$

16. $0 = a(-4 - (-2))^2 + 2$
$a = -\frac{1}{2}$
$y = -\frac{1}{2}(x + 2)^2 + 2$

Answers

17. $0 = a(-3 - (-2))^2 - 3$
$a = 3$
$y = 3(x + 2)^2 - 3$

18. $0 = a(2 - 3)^2 + 1$
$a = -1$
$y = -(x - 3)^2 + 1$

19. $4 = a(2 - 4)^2 + 0$
$a = 1$
$y = (x - 4)^2$

20. $0 = a(-3 - (-1))^2 - 3$
$a = \frac{3}{4}$
$y = \frac{3}{4}(x + 1)^2 - 3$

21A: $3 = a(-2 - (-3))^2 + 1$
$a = 2$
$y = 2(x + 3)^2 + 1$

B: $-1 = a(0 - (-2))^2 - 3$
$a = \frac{1}{2}$
$y = \frac{1}{2}(x + 2)^2 - 3$

C: $-5 = a(2 - 4)^2 - 1$
$a = -1$
$y = -(x - 4)^2 - 1$

22a. $x + 2 ; x + 2$
$x^2 + 4x + 4$
$x^2 + 4x - 1$

b. $y = 2(x^2 - 8x + 16) + 7$
$y = 2x^2 - 16x + 32 + 7$
$y = 2x^2 - 16x + 39$

23a. $y = (x^2 + 2x + 1 - 1) + 3$
$y = (x^2 + 2x + 1) - 1 + 3$
$y = (x + 1)^2 + 2$

b. $y = 3(x^2 + 4x) - 9$
$y = 3(x^2 + 4x + 4 - 4) - 9$
$y = 3(x^2 + 4x + 4) - 12 - 9$
$y = 3(x + 2)^2 - 21$

24. $y = x^2 + 4x + 4 - 3$
$y = x^2 + 4x + 1$
vertex: (-2,-3)
y-intercept: 1
opens upward

25. $y = -5(x^2 - 2x) - 4$
$y = -5(x^2 - 2x + 1 - 1) - 4$
$y = -5(x^2 - 2x + 1) + 5 - 4$
$y = -5(x - 1)^2 + 1$
vertex: (1,1)
y-intercept: -4
opens downward

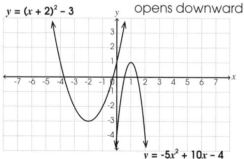

$y = (x + 2)^2 - 3$

$y = -5x^2 + 10x - 4$

26a. (-3,-5) ; $x = -3$; -5 ; min. ; upward ; 4
b. (3,10) ; $x = 3$; 10 ; max. ; downward ; 1
c. (-5,0) ; $x = -5$; 0 ; min. ; upward ; 50
d. (4,1) ; $x = 4$; 1 ; max. ; downward ; -15
e. (2,4) ; $x = 2$; 4 ; min. ; upward ; 6
f. (4,3) ; $x = 4$; 3 ; max. ; downward ; -77

27a. $y = x^2 - 8x + 17$
b. $y = -3x^2 - 18x - 27$
c. $y = 2x^2 - 4x - 3$
d. $y = 2(x + 3)^2$
e. $y = (x - 1)^2 - 2$
f. $y = -3(x - 2)^2 + 1$

28a. $y = \frac{1}{2}(x - 2)^2 - 1$
b. $y = -3(x + 3)^2 + 3$
c. $y = \frac{3}{2}(x - 4)^2$

29a. $y = -3x^2 + 18x - 29$
b. $y = -2x^2 - 4x + 5$
c. $y = -2x^2 + 28x - 80$
d. $y = x^2 - 4x - 32$

30. When written in standard form, the y-intercept of a quadratic relation can be determined by inspection. When written in vertex form, the vertex can be determined by inspection.

31. If a is zero in either standard form or vertex form, the x^2 term is zero. Without an x^2 term, the relation is not quadratic.

32. Graph B represents the arch because it has a y-intercept of 20 and opens downward.

33. $y = -0.2x^2 - 0.8x + 4.2$

34. Its domain is all real numbers and its range is all real numbers equal to or less than 1.

2.4 Applications

1.

2.

1 ; 5
4 ; 3 ; 1 ; 3 ; 5
-1
$-(x - 1)(x - 5)$

-2 ; 3
-3 ; 1 ; 2 ; 1 ; 3
$\frac{1}{2}$
$\frac{1}{2}(x + 2)(x - 3)$

3a.

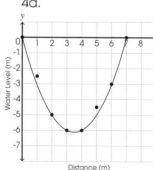

b. $y = a(x - 6)^2 + 16$
$0 = a(2 - 6)^2 + 16$
$a = -1$
$y = -(x - 6)^2 + 16$
c. $y = -(4.5 - 6)^2 + 16$
$y = 13.75$
The height was about 13.75 m.

4a.

b. $y = a(x - 0)(x - 7)$
$-6 = a(3 - 0)(3 - 7)$
$a = \frac{1}{2}$
$y = \frac{1}{2}x(x - 7)$
c. $-5 = \frac{1}{2}x(x - 7)$
$0 = x^2 - 7x + 10$
$0 = (x - 2)(x - 5)$
$x-2 = 0$ or $x-5 = 0$
$x = 2 \qquad x = 5$

The distance travelled was 2 m or 5 m.

5a. It is 20 m above
    ground.
  b. $y = a(x - 60)^2 + 20$
     $52 = a(100-60)^2+20$
     $52 = 1600a + 20$
     $a = \frac{1}{50}$
     $y = \frac{1}{50}(x - 60)^2 + 20$

6. $y = a(x - 0)^2 - 5$
    $-15 = a(10 - 0)^2 - 5$
    $-15 = 100a - 5$
    $a = -\frac{1}{10}$
    $y = -\frac{1}{10}x^2 - 5$

7a. $y = a(x - 10)^2 + 32$
     $0 = a(0 - 10)^2 + 32$
     $a = -\frac{8}{25}$
     $y = -\frac{8}{25}(x - 10)^2 + 32$

  b. $24 = -\frac{8}{25}(x - 10)^2 + 32$
     $25 = (x - 10)^2$
     $x = 10 \pm 5$
     $x = 5$ and $x = 15$
     $15 - 5 = 10$
     The width is 10 m.

8a. $P = -0.8x^2 + 56x - 480$
     $P = -0.8(x^2 - 70x) - 480$
     $P = -0.8(x^2 - 70x + 1225 - 1225) - 480$
     $P = -0.8(x - 35)^2 + 500$
  b. The maximum profit is $500.
  c. $0 = -0.8(x - 35)^2 + 500$
     $625 = (x - 35)^2$
     $x = 35 \pm 25$
     $x = 10$ and $x = 60$
     The cost of $10 or $60 will result in a profit
     of $0.

9a. $C = 0.2n^2 - 16n + 330$
     $C = 0.2(n^2 - 80n) + 330$
     $C = 0.2(n^2 - 80n + 1600 - 1600) + 330$
     $C = 0.2(n - 40)^2 + 10$
     40 figurines should be produced.
  b. $30 = 0.2(n - 40)^2 + 10$
     $100 = (n - 40)^2$
     $n = 40 \pm 10$
     $n = 30$ and $n = 50$
     30 or 50 figurines produced will lead to an
     average cost of $30.

10a. $h = -5t^2 + 10t + 3$
     $h = -5(t^2 - 2t) + 3$
     $h = -5(t^2-2t+1-1)+3$
     $h = -5(t - 1)^2 + 8$
     It was 8 m above water.
   b. $h = -5(0 - 1)^2 + 8$
      $h = 3$
      It is 3 m high.

11a. $2n$; $100n$
   b. $R = (4 + 2n)(800 - 100n)$
      $R = -200n^2 + 1200n + 3200$
      $R = -200(n^2 - 6n) + 3200$
      $R = -200(n^2 - 6n + 9 - 9) + 3200$
      $R = -200(n - 3)^2 + 5000$
   c. The maximum revenue is $5000.
   d. $4 + $2 x 3 = $10
      The ticket price of $10 will maximize
      revenue.

12a. Let R be the revenue and n be the number
     of $0.25 increases.
     $R = (3 + 0.25n)(1000 - 50n)$
  b. $R = -12.5n^2 + 100n + 3000$
     $R = -12.5(n^2 - 8n) + 3000$
     $R = -12.5(n^2 - 8n + 16 - 16) + 3000$
     $R = -12.5(n - 4)^2 + 3200$
  c. The greatest revenue is $3200.
  d. $3 + $0.25 x 4 = $4
     The price of $4 will result in the greatest
     revenue.

13a.

  b. A: $y = 0.5(x - 2)(x + 4)$
      $y = 0.5(x + 1)^2 - 4.5$

      B: $y = -(x - 1)(x + 3)$
      $y = -(x + 1)^2 + 4$

14a. It was 5 m.   b. It was 1 m.
   c. $y = -(x - 2)^2 + 5$
15a. It was 182 m.   b. It was 2 m.
   c. The flare was in the air for about 12 s.
16a. It will take 4 s.   b. It is 256 m.
   c. It will take 8 s.
17. The revenue will be maximized at $3.50.
18. The price of $1000 will maximize revenue.

Quiz 2

1. D   2. D   3. C   4. B
5. A   6. D   7. C   8. C
9. 0 ; (1 ; 1) ; downward ; $x = 1$; 1 ; max.
    -4 and 2 ; (-1,-9) ; upward ; $x = -1$; -9 ; min.
    -21 ; none ; (-4,-5) ; downward ; $x = -4$; -5 ; max.
    5 ; (-1,3) ; upward ; $x = -1$; 3 ; min.
    6 ; none ; (-5,1) ; upward ; $x = -5$; 1 ; min.
10a. zeros: 3, -1 ; opens upward ; D
   b. vertex: (-1,4) ; opens upward ; E
   c. y-intercept: 3 ; opens upward ; F
   d. zeros: -3, 1 ; opens downward ; A
   e. y-intercept: -5 ; opens upward ; C
   f. vertex: (1,-4) ; opens downward ; B
11. A: vertex form: B: factored form:
        $y = a(x - 1)^2 + 4$ $y = a(x + 1)(x - 1)$
        $3 = a(0 - 1)^2 + 4$ $2 = a(0 + 1)(0 - 1)$
        $a = -1$ $a = -2$
        $y = -(x - 1)^2 + 4$ $y = -2(x + 1)(x - 1)$
        standard form: vertex form:
        $y = -(x - 1)^2 + 4$ $y = -2(x - 0)^2 + 2$
        $y = -(x^2 - 2x + 1) + 4$ $y = -2x^2 + 2$
        $y = -x^2 + 2x + 3$

Answers

12. $y = a(x - 7)^2 + 23$
$5 = a(4 - 7)^2 + 23$
$a = -2$
$y = -2(x - 7)^2 + 23$

13. $y = a(x - 4)(x + 2)$
$5 = a(1 - 4)(1 + 2)$
$a = -\dfrac{5}{9}$
$y = -\dfrac{5}{9}(x - 4)(x + 2)$

14. $y = a(x + 3)^2 + 8$
$-7 = a(0 + 3)^2 + 8$
$a = -\dfrac{5}{3}$
$y = -\dfrac{5}{3}(x + 3)^2 + 8$
$y = -\dfrac{5}{3}x^2 - 10x - 7$

15. axis of symmetry: $x = -2$
$y = a(x + 3)(x + 1)$
$-2 = a(-2 + 3)(-2 + 1)$
$a = 2$
$y = 2(x + 3)(x + 1)$
$y = 2x^2 + 8x + 6$

16. B ; C ; A

17. $y = a(x - 3)^2 + 1$
$4 = a(0 - 3)^2 + 1$
$a = \dfrac{1}{3}$
$y = \dfrac{1}{3}(x - 3)^2 + 1$

18. $y = a(x + 1)(x - 3)$
$2 = a(1 + 1)(1 - 3)$
$a = -\dfrac{1}{2}$
$y = -\dfrac{1}{2}(x + 1)(x - 3)$

19. -8

20. (-2,6)

21. (-4,-7)

22a.
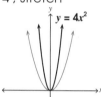
Height (m) / Distance (m)

b. $y = a(x - 0)(x - 3)$
$y = ax(x - 3)$
$2 = a(1)(1 - 3)$
$a = -1$
$y = -x(x - 3)$

23a. $h = -0.01d^2 + 0.4d + 2$
$h = -0.01(d^2 - 40d) + 2$
$h = -0.01(d^2 - 40d + 400 - 400) + 2$
$h = -0.01(d - 20)^2 + 6$
The maximum height of the ball was 6 m.

b. $0 = -0.01(d - 20)^2 + 6$
$600 = (d - 20)^2$
$d = 20 \pm \sqrt{600}$
$d = -4.495$ or 44.495
It landed 44.495 m downfield.

24. Let R be the revenue and n be the number of $0.10 reduction in price.
$R = (8 - 0.1n)(640 + 40n)$
$R = -4n^2 + 256n + 5120$
$R = -4(n^2 - 64n) + 5120$
$R = -4(n^2 - 64n + 1024 - 1024) + 5120$
$R = -4(n - 32)^2 + 9216$
$8 - \$0.1 \times 32 = \$4.80$
It should charge \$4.80 to maximize revenue.
9216 sandwiches will be sold at this price.

25. For a quadratic equation that opens downward, if it has a maximum that is less than zero, then it will result in no zeros.

26. The axis of symmetry can be found by:
- in standard form, $y = ax^2 + bx + c$, $x = -\dfrac{b}{2a}$
- in vertex form, $y = a(x - h)^2 + k$, $x = h$
- in factored form, $y = a(x - r)(x - s)$, $x = \dfrac{r + s}{2}$

27. $y = a(x - 0)^2 + 192$
$0 = a(96 - 0)^2 + 192$
$a = -\dfrac{1}{48}$
$y = -\dfrac{1}{48}x^2 + 192$

28. $-4 = a(-5 + 3)^2 + k$ $20 = a(1 + 3)^2 + k$
$0 = 4a + 4 + k$ $0 = 16a - 20 + k$
$4a + 4 + k = 16a - 20 + k$
$a = 2$
$0 = 4(2) + 4 + k$
$k = -12$
So, $y = 2(x + 3)^2 - 12$.

Chapter 3: Transformations

3.1 Stretches/Compressions and Reflections

1a. 3 ; 0 ; 3 ; B ; stretched ; 3
b. 3 ; 0 ; 3 ; A ; compressed ; $\dfrac{1}{3}$
c. -3 ; 0 ; -3 ; D ; stretched ; 3
d. -3 ; 0 ; -3 ; C ; compressed ; $\dfrac{1}{3}$

2. 4 ; stretch
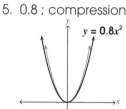
$y = 4x^2$

3. 0.2 ; compression
$y = 0.2x^2$

4. 1.5 ; stretch
$y = 1.5x^2$

5. 0.8 ; compression
$y = 0.8x^2$

6. upward ; downward ; $y = 2x^2$; $y = -x^2$
7. downward ; upward ; $y = \dfrac{1}{4}x^2$; $y = -\dfrac{1}{2}x^2$

8a. stretch
downward
b. compression
upward
c. compression
upward
d. stretch
downward

8-9.
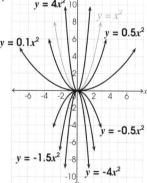
$y = 4x^2$; $y = x^2$; $y = 0.5x^2$; $y = 0.1x^2$; $y = -0.5x^2$; $y = -1.5x^2$; $y = -4x^2$

10.
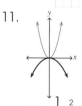
$4x^2$

11.
$y = -\dfrac{1}{4}x^2$

12.
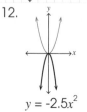
$y = -2.5x^2$

13a. B ; A ; C   b. A ; C ; B   c. A ; C ; B

14.

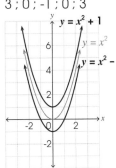

15. (Suggested answers)
   a. 0.5
   b. 2
   c. -0.3

16a. $y = \frac{1}{5}x^2$

   b. $y = -\frac{1}{5}x^2$

   c. $y = 2x^2$

   d. (Suggested answer)
     $y = -1.5x^2$

10. The vertex of the relation is equal to (h,k).
11. (-2,-1)   12. (2,-1)   13. (1,2)   14. (1,-2)

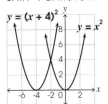
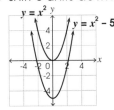

15a. $y = x^2 - 3$ b. $y = (x + 2)^2$ c. $y = x^2 + 2$
16a. B   b. F   c. C   d. E   e. A   f. D
17a. shift 5 units down   b. shift 4 units left

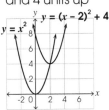
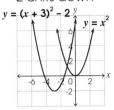

c. shift 2 units right   d. shift 3 units left and
   and 4 units up   2 units down

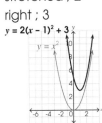
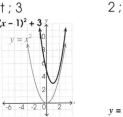

18a. $y = (x - 5)^2 - 1$ b. $y = (x + 4)^2 + 3$

3.2 Translations

1. 5 ; 2 ; 1 ; 2 ; 5
   3 ; 0 ; -1 ; 0 ; 3

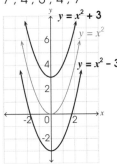

2. 1 ; -2 ; -3 ; -2 ; 1
   7 ; 4 ; 3 ; 4 ; 7

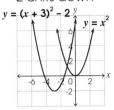

a. 1
b. 1

3. translates up
4. translates down

a. 3 ; down
b. 3 ; up

3-4.

5. 4 ; 0 ; 4
   4 ; 0 ; 4
a. 2 units right
b. translates 2 units
   left

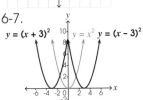

6. translates right
7. translates left

6-7.

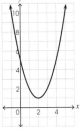

3.3 Transformation with Vertex Form

1. 11 ; 5 ; 3 ; 5 ; 11
   upward
   stretched ; 2
   right ; 3

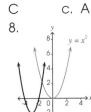

2. -5 ; -2 ; -1 ; -2 ; -5
   downward
   compressed ; $\frac{1}{4}$
   2 ; left ; down

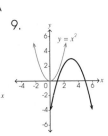

3a. stretch   b. compression
  c. upward   d. downward
4a. right   b. left
5a. up   b. down
   vertex: h ; k
6a. B   b. C   c. A

8. 10
   5
   2
   1
   2
   5
   10
   (2,1)

9. 7
   2
   -1
   -2
   -1
   2
   7
   (-1,-2)

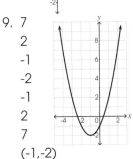

7.

8.

9.

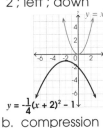

Answers

10. 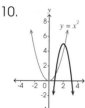 11. 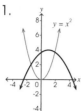 12.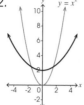

13. A: $y = 5(x + 6)^2$ B: $y = -0.25(x + 4)^2 + 6$
    C: $y = -3(x - 5)^2 + 2$

14a. B   b. D   c. A   d. C

15a. $y = \dfrac{2}{5}(x + 3)^2$ b. $y = 9x^2 - 4$
    c. $y = -(x - 3)^2 + 3$ d. $y = \dfrac{1}{2}(x + 2)^2 + 4$
    e. $y = -(x - 2)^2 - 0.5$

16a. 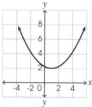   b.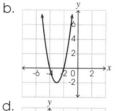

c.   d.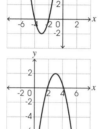

17a. $y = 3(x + 2)^2 - 6$ b. $y = \dfrac{1}{3}(x - 3)^2 + 2$

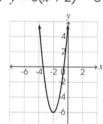   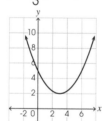

Quiz 3

1. C   2. D   3. A   4. C
5a. B   b. D   6. A   7. A
8. A   9. B   10. B   11. A
12. B ; A ; C   13. B ; C ; A
14. vertically stretched by a factor of 3 and translate 9 units up
15. reflect in the x-axis, vertically compressed by a factor of $\dfrac{1}{3}$, and translate 4 units up
16. translate 7 units left and 2 units up
17. vertically stretched by a factor of 5 and translate 3 units right and 9 units down
18. reflect in the x-axis, vertically compressed by a factor of $\dfrac{5}{8}$, and translate 2 units left and 1 unit down

19. reflect in the x-axis and translate $\dfrac{1}{2}$ unit right and $\dfrac{4}{3}$ units up
20. $-(x + 3)^2 + 5$ 21. $y = \dfrac{1}{2}(x - 5)^2$
22. $y = 10(x + 5)^2 - 2$ 23. $y = -3x^2 - 5$
24a. $y = -(x + 3)^2 + 5$ and $y = -3x^2 - 5$
    b. $y = \dfrac{1}{2}(x - 5)^2$ c. $y = -3x^2 - 5$
    d. $y = -(x + 3)^2 + 5$ e. $y = 10(x + 5)^2 - 2$
    f. $y = 10(x + 5)^2 - 2$

25. 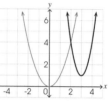   26.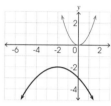

27. 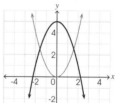   28.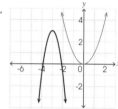

29. $y = 2x^2 + 8x + 10$
    $y = 2(x^2 + 4x) + 10$
    $y = 2(x^2 + 4x + 4 - 4) + 10$
    $y = 2(x + 2)^2 + 2$

30. $y = -\dfrac{1}{2}x^2 + 4x - 8$
    $y = -\dfrac{1}{2}(x^2 - 8x + 16)$
    $y = -\dfrac{1}{2}(x - 4)^2$

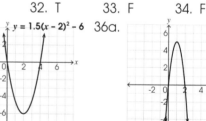

31. T   32. T   33. F   34. F

35a.   36a.

b. He reached a depth of 6 m.   b. It was 5 m.
c. It took 2 seconds.   c. It took 1 second.

37a. The parabola is vertically stretched and reflected in the x-axis.
    b. The parabola is vertically compressed.
    c. The parabola is vertically stretched.

38. The value of h does not affect the number of zeros. If the signs of a and k are different, then there are two zeros. If the signs of a and k are the same, then there are no zeros. If k is 0, then there is exactly one zero regardless of a.

39. (Suggested answer)

    If the parabola is translated 7 units right and 12 units up, its equation is $y = (x-7)^2 + 12$. If the parabola is translated 5 units right and 8 units up from (2,4) to (7,12), the equation is $y = (x-5)^2 + 8$.

40. $y = a(x-3)^2 + 6$

    $y = ax^2 - 6ax + 9a + 6$

    $ax^2 + bx + 12 = ax^2 - 6ax + 9a + 6$

    $12 = 9a + 6$ $b = -6a$

    $a = \dfrac{2}{3}$ $b = -6 \times \dfrac{2}{3} = -4$

    So, a is $\dfrac{2}{3}$ and b is -4.

Chapter 4: Quadratic Equations

4.1 Solving Quadratic Equations

1. 1 ; 2   2. 1 ; 2   3. 1 ; 2
     1 ; 2   1 ; 2   1 ; 2
     -1 ; -2   -0.5 ; -2   0.5 ; 2

4. $(x+1)(x+4) = 0$

    $x + 1 = 0$ or $x + 4 = 0$

       $x = -1$ $x = -4$

5. $x(x+6) = 0$ 6. $(x+3)(x-2) = 0$

    $x = 0$ or $x + 6 = 0$ $x + 3 = 0$ or $x - 2 = 0$

             $x = -6$ $x = -3$ $x = 2$

7. $(x+3)(x-8) = 0$ 8. $(2x+3)(x+2) = 0$

    $x+3 = 0$ or $x-8 = 0$ $2x + 3 = 0$ or $x + 2 = 0$

       $x = -3$ $x = 8$ $x = -1.5$ $x = -2$

9. $3(x^2 + 5x + 4) = 0$ 10. $2(2x^2 + 5x + 2) = 0$

    $3(x+1)(x+4) = 0$ $2(2x+1)(x+2) = 0$

    $x+1 = 0$ or $x+4 = 0$ $2x + 1 = 0$ or $x + 2 = 0$

       $x = -1$ $x = -4$ $x = -0.5$ $x = -2$

11. $(x+5)^2 = 0$ 12. $2(4x^2 - 4x + 1) = 0$

       $x + 5 = 0$ $2(2x-1)^2 = 0$

         $x = -5$ $2x - 1 = 0$

                          $x = 0.5$

13. $x^2 + 4x - 5 = 0$ 14. $x^2 - 3x - 10 = 0$

    $(x+5)(x-1) = 0$ $(x+2)(x-5) = 0$

    $x+5 = 0$ or $x-1 = 0$ $x + 2 = 0$ or $x - 5 = 0$

      $x = -5$ $x = 1$ $x = -2$ $x = 5$

15. $3x^2 + 2x - 1 = 0$ 16. $4x^2 - 6x + 2 = 0$

    $(3x-1)(x+1) = 0$ $2(2x^2 - 3x + 1) = 0$

    $3x-1 = 0$ or $x+1 = 0$ $2(2x-1)(x-1) = 0$

    $x = \dfrac{1}{3}$ $x = -1$ $2x - 1 = 0$ or $x - 1 = 0$

                        $x = 0.5$ $x = 1$

17. $3x^2 - 6x + 3 = 0$ 18. $(2x+7)(x-2) = 0$

    $3(x^2 - 2x + 1) = 0$ $2x + 7 = 0$ or $x - 2 = 0$

       $3(x-1)^2 = 0$ $x = -3.5$ $x = 2$

         $x - 1 = 0$ -3.5 ; -3.5 ; 0

           $x = 1$ 2 ; 2 ; 0

19-23. (Individual answer checking)

19. $3x^2 + 11x + 6 = 0$ $3x + 2 = 0$ or $x + 3 = 0$

    $(3x+2)(x+3) = 0$ $x = -\dfrac{2}{3}$ $x = -3$

20. $2x^2 - 7x + 6 = 0$ $2x - 3 = 0$ or $x - 2 = 0$

    $(2x-3)(x-2) = 0$ $x = 1.5$ $x = 2$

21. $-10x^2 + 32x - 6 = 0$ $5x - 1 = 0$ or $x - 3 = 0$

    $-2(5x^2 - 16x + 3) = 0$ $x = 0.2$ $x = 3$

    $-2(5x-1)(x-3) = 0$

22. $6x^2 + 15x - 9 = 0$ $2x - 1 = 0$ or $x + 3 = 0$

    $3(2x^2 + 5x - 3) = 0$ $x = 0.5$ $x = -3$

    $3(2x-1)(x+3) = 0$

23. $9x^2 + 12x + 4 = 0$

        $(3x+2)^2 = 0$

          $3x + 2 = 0$

            $x = -\dfrac{2}{3}$

24. $x^2 + 2x + 1 = 16$ 25. $x^2 + 6x = 0$

    $x^2 + 2x - 15 = 0$ $x(x+6) = 0$

    $(x-3)(x+5) = 0$ $x = 0$ or $x + 6 = 0$

    $x - 3 = 0$ or $x + 5 = 0$ $x = -6$

       $x = 3$ $x = -5$

26. $3x^2 = 10x + 8$ 27. $4x^2 + 20x + 13 = 3x + 90$

    $3x^2 - 10x - 8 = 0$ $4x^2 + 17x - 77 = 0$

    $(3x+2)(x-4) = 0$ $(4x-11)(x+7) = 0$

    $3x+2 = 0$ or $x-4 = 0$ $4x-11 = 0$ or $x+7 = 0$

    $x = -\dfrac{2}{3}$ $x = 4$ $x = 2.75$ $x = -7$

28. $10x^2 + 2x - 73 = 9x^2 + 8x - 1$

    $x^2 - 6x - 72 = 0$

    $(x+6)(x-12) = 0$

    $x + 6 = 0$ or $x - 12 = 0$

       $x = -6$ $x = 12$

29. $4x^2 + 10x + 8 = -2x^2 - 3x + 2$

      $6x^2 + 13x + 6 = 0$

      $(3x+2)(2x+3) = 0$

      $3x + 2 = 0$ or $2x + 3 = 0$

        $x = -\dfrac{2}{3}$ $x = -\dfrac{3}{2}$

30a. $2(5)^2 + 9(5) - 5 = 90$ b. $2(\dfrac{3}{2})^2 + 5(\dfrac{3}{2}) - 12 = 0$

    5 is not a root. $\dfrac{3}{2}$ is a root.

31a. $x = 3$ or $x = 5$ b. $x = 0$ or $x = \dfrac{1}{3}$

    $x - 3 = 0$ $x - 5 = 0$ $3x - 1 = 0$

    $(x-3)(x-5) = 0$ $x(3x-1) = 0$

    $x^2 - 8x + 15 = 0$ $3x^2 - x = 0$

32. 0 and 2   33. 3

    $x^2 - 2x + 1 - 1 = 0$ $x - 3 = 0$

        $x^2 - 2x = 0$ $x = 3$

        $x(x-2) = 0$ 3

       $x = 0$ or $x = 2$

    0 and 2

Answers

34. -4 and 0
$$x^2 + 4x + 4 - 4 = 0$$
$$x^2 + 4x = 0$$
$$x(x + 4) = 0$$
$$x = -4 \text{ or } x = 0$$
-4 and 0

35. -1 and 1
$$-2(x^2 - 1) = 0$$
$$-2(x + 1)(x - 1) = 0$$
$$x = -1 \text{ or } x = 1$$
-1 and 1

36. The zeros of the graphs and the roots of the corresponding equations are the same.

37. She should look for the zeros of the graph to find the solution.

38a. -2 and 1   b. -3 and -4   c. 5 and 2
d. -0.5 and 3   e. -1 and $\frac{2}{3}$ f. -0.2 and -2.5
g. -1 and -3.5   h. 6 and $-\frac{1}{3}$ i. -8 and 0.75
j. -2.5 and 0.25

39a. 6 and 7   b. 12 and -4   c. -5 and -3
d. $\frac{8}{3}$ and -1   e. -1.5 and 1.25   f. -4 and 0.25
g. 5 and 0   h. -8 and 8   i. -1 and -0.625
j. 4.5 and -1

40a. -2   b. -3 and 1
c. 1 and 5   d. -6 and -4

41a. -1 and 2   b. -8 and 2.5   c. $-\frac{1}{7}$ and 2.5
d. -7 and $-\frac{7}{3}$ e. -7 and 2.75   f. -1 and 4

42a. no   b. yes   c. no   d. yes

43. (Suggested answers)
a. $x^2 - 3x - 4 = 0$ b. $x^2 + 9x + 14 = 0$
c. $18x^2 - 9x + 1 = 0$ d. $25x^2 - 40x + 16 = 0$
e. $3x^2 - x - 10 = 0$ f. $4x^2 + 28x + 45 = 0$

44. No. The quadratic equations have the same axis of symmetry but may have different directions of opening.

45. If a quadratic equation cannot be written in the factored form, then it cannot be solved by factoring.

46. No. When $y = x^2 - 3x + 1$ is graphed, its parabola crosses the x-axis at two points, which are the two x-intercepts. Although the quadratic equation $x^2 - 3x + 1 = 0$ is not factorable over the integers, it does have two solutions (the two x-intercepts).

4.2 Quadratic Formula

1. 1 ; -2 ; 3 ; B   2. -1 ; 5 ; -4 ; A
3. 2 ; -3 ; 4 ; B   4. -5 ; 1 ; 0 ; B

5. $\dfrac{-4 \pm \sqrt{4^2 - 4(1)(3)}}{2(1)}$; $\dfrac{-4 \pm \sqrt{4}}{2}$
$\dfrac{-4 + 2}{2} = -1$; $\dfrac{-4 - 2}{2} = -3$

6. $x = \dfrac{-3 \pm \sqrt{3^2 - 4(1)(-4)}}{2(1)}$
$x = \dfrac{-3 \pm \sqrt{25}}{2}$
$x = \dfrac{-3 \pm 5}{2}$
$x = \dfrac{-3 + 5}{2} = 1$ or $x = \dfrac{-3 - 5}{2} = -4$

7. $x = \dfrac{-(-10) \pm \sqrt{(-10)^2 - 4(-1)(-9)}}{2(-1)}$
$x = \dfrac{10 \pm \sqrt{64}}{-2}$
$x = \dfrac{10 \pm 8}{-2}$
$x = \dfrac{10 + 8}{-2} = -9$ or $x = \dfrac{10 - 8}{-2} = -1$

8. $x = \dfrac{-3 \pm \sqrt{3^2 - 4(2)(-2)}}{2(2)}$
$x = \dfrac{-3 \pm \sqrt{25}}{4}$
$x = \dfrac{-3 \pm 5}{4}$
$x = \dfrac{-3 + 5}{4} = 0.5$ or $x = \dfrac{-3 - 5}{4} = -2$

9. $2(x^2 - 2x - 3) = 0$
$x = \dfrac{-(-2) \pm \sqrt{(-2)^2 - 4(1)(-3)}}{2(1)}$
$x = \dfrac{2 \pm \sqrt{16}}{2}$
$x = \dfrac{2 \pm 4}{2}$
$x = \dfrac{2 + 4}{2} = 3$ or $x = \dfrac{2 - 4}{2} = -1$

10. $x = \dfrac{-(-8) \pm \sqrt{(-8)^2 - 4(4)(3)}}{2(4)}$
$x = \dfrac{8 \pm \sqrt{16}}{8}$
$x = \dfrac{8 \pm 4}{8}$
$x = \dfrac{8 + 4}{8} = 1.5$ or $x = \dfrac{8 - 4}{8} = 0.5$

11. $3(x^2 + 7x + 6) = 0$
$x = \dfrac{-7 \pm \sqrt{7^2 - 4(1)(6)}}{2(1)}$
$x = \dfrac{-7 \pm \sqrt{25}}{2}$
$x = \dfrac{-7 \pm 5}{2}$
$x = \dfrac{-7 + 5}{2} = -1$ or $x = \dfrac{-7 - 5}{2} = -6$

12. $4x^2 + 20x + 25 = 0$
$x = \dfrac{-20 \pm \sqrt{20^2 - 4(4)(25)}}{2(4)}$
$x = \dfrac{-20 \pm \sqrt{0}}{8}$
$x = \dfrac{-20}{8}$
$x = -2.5$

13. $3x^2 - 8x + 1 = 0$
$x = \dfrac{-(-8) \pm \sqrt{(-8)^2 - 4(3)(1)}}{2(3)}$
$x = \dfrac{8 \pm \sqrt{52}}{6}$
$x \doteq 2.54$ and $x \doteq 0.13$

14. $4 - 5x^2 = 5x + 5$
$-5x^2 - 5x - 1 = 0$
$x = \dfrac{-(-5) \pm \sqrt{(-5)^2 - 4(-5)(-1)}}{2(-5)}$
$x = \dfrac{5 \pm \sqrt{5}}{-10}$
$x \doteq -0.72$ and $x \doteq -0.28$

15. $7x^2 + 8x + 1 = 0$
$x = \dfrac{-8 \pm \sqrt{8^2 - 4(7)(1)}}{2(7)}$
$x = \dfrac{-8 \pm \sqrt{36}}{14}$
$x = \dfrac{-8 \pm 6}{14}$
$x \doteq -0.14$ and $x = -1$

16. $x^2 - 8x + 12 = 3x^2 + 3x$
$-2x^2 - 11x + 12 = 0$
$x = \dfrac{-(-11) \pm \sqrt{(-11)^2 - 4(-2)(12)}}{2(-2)}$
$x = \dfrac{11 \pm \sqrt{217}}{-4}$
$x \doteq -6.43$ and $x \doteq 0.93$

17. $x^2 + x = -4x^2 + 12x$
$5x^2 - 11x = 0$
$x = \dfrac{-(-11) \pm \sqrt{(-11)^2 - 4(5)(0)}}{2(5)}$
$x = \dfrac{11 \pm 11}{10}$
$x = 0$ and $x = 2.2$

18. $x^2 - 4x + 4 = 5x^2$
$-4x^2 - 4x + 4 = 0$
$x = \dfrac{-(-4) \pm \sqrt{(-4)^2 - 4(-4)(4)}}{2(-4)}$
$x = \dfrac{4 \pm \sqrt{80}}{-8}$
$x \doteq -1.62$ and $x \doteq 0.62$

19. $4x^2 + 4x + 1 = -25x^2 - 40x - 16 + 2$
$29x^2 + 44x + 15 = 0$
$x = \dfrac{-44 \pm \sqrt{44^2 - 4(29)(15)}}{2(29)}$
$x = \dfrac{-44 \pm \sqrt{196}}{58}$
$x = \dfrac{-44 \pm 14}{58}$
$x = -1$ and $x \doteq -0.52$

20. $x^2 - 2x - 1 = 0$
$x = \dfrac{-(-2) \pm \sqrt{(-2)^2 - 4(1)(-1)}}{2(1)}$
$x = \dfrac{2 \pm \sqrt{8}}{2}$
$x \doteq 2.41$ and $x \doteq -0.41$

21. $x^2 + 6x + 7 = 0$
$x = \dfrac{-6 \pm \sqrt{6^2 - 4(1)(7)}}{2(1)}$
$x = \dfrac{-6 \pm \sqrt{8}}{2}$
$x \doteq -4.41$ and $x \doteq -1.59$

22. $2x^2 + x - 2 = 0$
$x = \dfrac{-1 \pm \sqrt{1^2 - 4(2)(-2)}}{2(2)}$
$x = \dfrac{-1 \pm \sqrt{17}}{4}$
$x \doteq -1.28$ and $x \doteq 0.78$

23. $-x^2 + 7x - 9 = 0$
$x = \dfrac{-7 \pm \sqrt{7^2 - 4(-1)(-9)}}{2(-1)}$
$x = \dfrac{-7 \pm \sqrt{13}}{-2}$
$x \doteq 5.30$ and $x \doteq 1.70$

24. $3x^2 - 4x - 3 = 0$
$x = \dfrac{-(-4) \pm \sqrt{(-4)^2 - 4(3)(-3)}}{2(3)}$
$x = \dfrac{4 \pm \sqrt{52}}{6}$
$x \doteq 1.87$ and $x \doteq -0.54$

25. $-4x^2 - 2x = 0$
$x = \dfrac{-(-2) \pm \sqrt{(-2)^2 - 4(-4)(0)}}{2(-4)}$
$x = \dfrac{2 \pm \sqrt{4}}{-8}$
$x = -0.5$ and $x = 0$

A: $3x^2 - 4x - 3$ B: $y = -x^2 + 7x - 9$
C: $y = -4x^2 - 2x$ D: $y = x^2 + 6x + 7$
E: $y = x^2 - 2x - 1$ F: $y = 2x^2 + x - 2$

26. $(x - 9)^2 = 0$ | $x = \dfrac{-(-18) \pm \sqrt{(-18)^2 - 4(1)(81)}}{2(1)}$
$x - 9 = 0$ | $x = \dfrac{18 \pm \sqrt{0}}{2}$
$x = 9$ | $x = 9$

27. $-(2x - 1)(2x - 3) = 0$
$2x - 1 = 0$ or $2x - 3 = 0$
    $x = 0.5$ $x = 1.5$
$x = \dfrac{-8 \pm \sqrt{8^2 - 4(-4)(-3)}}{2(-4)}$
$x = \dfrac{-8 \pm \sqrt{16}}{-8}$
$x = \dfrac{-8 \pm 4}{-8}$
$x = 0.5$ and $x = 1.5$

28. If the factored form of the quadratic equation can be found easily, then solving it by factoring is preferred.

29. Applying the quadratic formula or graphing can be used to solve a quadratic equation that cannot be factored.

30. F   31a. T   b. F   c. T

32a. -4 and -1   b. 3 and -2   c. 3 and -1
   d. -6 and -1   e. 3.5 and 1   f. 2 and $\dfrac{2}{3}$
   g. $\dfrac{1 + \sqrt{33}}{8}$ and $\dfrac{1 - \sqrt{33}}{8}$
   h. $\dfrac{3 + \sqrt{6}}{3}$ and $\dfrac{3 - \sqrt{6}}{3}$

Answers

33a. 0.5 and 1.25   b. 1.17 and -0.28
   c. -3.5 and 0.67   d. 1.51 and -0.88
   e. -6 and 4   f. -2.49 and 1.29
34a. 3.79 and -0.79 ; B   b. -3.41 and -0.59 ; D
   c. 4.74 and 0.26 ; A   d. 2.44 and 0.16 ; C
35. Solving a quadratic equation by factoring is more efficient if the relation can be factored easily. However, factoring cannot be used for all equations. Solving by quadratic formula may take longer but can be used to solve all quadratic equations that have solutions.
36a. The equation is $y = (x + 2)^2 + 2$. Its vertex is (-2,2) and the parabola opens upward.
   b. He got an error because the graph does not have any zeros, implying that the equation has no solutions. So, it cannot be solved by any methods, including the quadratic formula.
37. They are (-1,-5) and (-0.5,-4).

4.3 Real Roots and Discriminants

1a. >   b. <   c. =   d. >
2a. 2   b. 1   c. 0   d. 0
   e. 2   f. 0
3. -9 ; 7 ; 2   4. $D = 8^2 - 4(2)(9)$
   81 ; 56 $= 64 - 72$
   25                              $= -8$
   2   no real roots
5. $D = 13^2 - 4(6)(-4)$ 6. $D = (-10)^2 - 4(25)(1)$
   $= 169 - (-96)$ $= 100 - 100$
   $= 265$ $= 0$
   2 real roots   1 real root
7. $3x^2 - 2x + 9 = 0$ 8. $D = 0^2 - 4(3)(-8)$
   $D = (-2)^2 - 4(3)(9)$ $= 0 - (-96)$
   $= 4 - 108$ $= 96$
   $= -104$ 2 real roots
   no real roots
9. $x^2 - 4x + 6 = 0$ 10. $2x^2 + 4x + 2 = 0$
   $D = (-4)^2 - 4(1)(6)$ $D = 4^2 - 4(2)(2)$
   $= 16 - 24$ $= 16 - 16$
   $= -8$ $= 0$
   no real roots   1 real root
11. $2x^2 - x - 6 = -x^2 + 8x - 16$
   $3x^2 - 9x + 10 = 0$
   $D = (-9)^2 - 4(3)(10)$
   $= 81 - 120$
   $= -39$
   no real roots

12a. $D = 2^2 - 4(1)(-3) = 16$; 2 x-intercepts
   b. $D = (-5)^2 - 4(2)(8) = -39$; no x-intercepts
   c. $D = (-8)^2 - 4(2)(8) = 0$; 1 x-intercept
   $2x^2 - 5x + 8$; $y = 2x^2 - 8x + 8$; $y = x^2 + 2x - 3$
13a. $D = 2^2 - 4(-2)(-1) = -4$; no x-intercepts
   b. $D = 5^2 - 4(-1)(-3) = 13$; 2 x-intercepts
   c. $D = 1.8^2 - 4(-0.5)(-1.62) = 0$; 1 x-intercept
   $-x^2 + 5x - 3$; $y = -2x^2 + 2x - 1$
   $y = -0.5x^2 + 1.8x - 1.62$
14a. $(-16)^2 - 4(1)(k) = 0$ b. $k^2 - 4(3)(12) = 0$
   $256 - 4k = 0$ $k^2 - 144 = 0$
   $4k = 256$ $k^2 = 144$
   $k = 64$ $k = \pm\sqrt{144}$
                                   $k = 12$ or -12
15a. $(-4)^2 - 4(k)(1) > 0$ b. $(-4)^2 - 4(k)(1) < 0$
   $16 - 4k > 0$ $16 - 4k < 0$
   $16 > 4k$ $16 < 4k$
   $4 > k$ $4 < k$
16a. 2   b. 0   c. 1   d. 0
17a. $D = 0$ b. $D < 0$ c. $D > 0$ or $D = 0$
18a. $D = 1$, 2 real roots   b. $D = -4$, no real roots
   c. $D = 0$, 1 real root   d. $D = -9$, no real roots
19a. no real roots   b. 2 real roots, $x = 5$ or -2
   c. 1 real root, $x = 1$ d. 2 real roots, $x = 1$ or -0.6
20a. no x-intercepts   b. -1.58 and 0.71
   c. no x-intercepts   d. 0.42 and 1.58
21a. $k = \sqrt{28}$ or $-\sqrt{28}$ b. $k = -49$
   c. $k = \dfrac{9}{8}$ d. $k = 6$
22a. $-4 < k < 4$ b. $k = -4$ or 4
   c. $k > 4$ or $k < -4$
23. A perfect-square trinomial has the form $a^2x^2 + 2abx + b^2$. The discriminant is $(2ab)^2 - 4(a^2)(b^2) = 4a^2b^2 - 4a^2b^2 = 0$. This shows that the discriminant is always zero for a perfect-square trinomial, and so it always has exactly one real root.
24. If the discriminant is 0 or greater, then the quadratic relation has x-intercepts; otherwise, it has no x-intercepts.
25. $D = (-2a)^2 - 4(a - b)(a + b)$
   $= 4a^2 - 4(a^2 - b^2)$
   $= 4a^2 - 4a^2 + 4b^2$
   $= 4b^2$
   Since $4b^2$ is always greater than 0, the quadratic equation has two real roots.
26. There are two points of intersection: (1,2) and (6,77).

4.4 Application of Quadratic Relations

1a. B   b. A   2a. A   b. A

3. $h = -5t^2 + 20t + 25$
   $h = -5(t^2 - 4t) + 25$
   $h = -5(t - 2)^2 + 45$
   The Frisbee's maximum height was 45 m.

4. $-5t^2 + 10t = 0$
   $-5t(t - 2) = 0$
   $t = 0$ or $t - 2 = 0$
                  $t = 2$
   $2 - 0 = 2$
   The ball was in the air for 2 seconds.

5. $0.1x^2 + 2.4x + 5 = 453$
   $0.1x^2 + 2.4x - 448 = 0$
   $x = \dfrac{-2.4 \pm \sqrt{2.4^2 - 4(0.1)(-448)}}{2(0.1)}$
   $x = \dfrac{-2.4 \pm 13.6}{0.2}$ cannot be negative ↓
   $x = \dfrac{-2.4 + 13.6}{0.2} = 56$ or $x = \dfrac{-2.4 - 13.6}{0.2} = -80$
   They can purchase 56 costumes for $453.

6. Let l be the length of the field.
   $l(100 - l) = 2275$
   $-l^2 + 100l - 2275 = 0$
   $x = \dfrac{-100 \pm \sqrt{100^2 - 4(-1)(-2275)}}{2(-1)}$
   $x = \dfrac{-100 \pm 30}{-2}$
   $x = \dfrac{-100 + 30}{-2} = 35$ or $x = \dfrac{-100 - 30}{-2} = 65$
   $100 - 35 = 65$ and $100 - 65 = 35$
   The dimensions of the field are 35 m and 65 m.

7. $-0.003x^2 + 12x + 27\ 760 = 40\ 000$
   $-0.003x^2 + 12x - 12\ 240 = 0$
   $D = 12^2 - 4(-0.003)(-12\ 240) = -2.88$
   There are no real roots. So, it is not possible.

8. Let R be the revenue and x be the number of $2 increases.
   $R = (36 + 2x)(360 - 10x)$
   $R = -20x^2 + 360x + 12\ 960$
   $R = -20(x^2 - 18x) + 12\ 960$
   $R = -20(x - 9)^2 + 14\ 580$
   The maximum revenue is $14 580.

9. Let R be the revenue and x be the number of $2 increases.
   $R = (20 + 2x)(1200 - 60x)$
   $R = -120x^2 + 1200x + 24\ 000$
   $-120x^2 + 1200x + 24\ 000 = 17\ 280$
      $-120x^2 + 1200x + 6720 = 0$
        $-120(x^2 - 10x - 56) = 0$
   $x = \dfrac{-(-10) \pm \sqrt{(-10)^2 - 4(1)(-56)}}{2(1)}$
   $x = \dfrac{10 \pm 18}{2}$
   $x = \dfrac{10 + 18}{2} = 14$ or $x = \dfrac{10 - 18}{2} = -4$
   Price with 14 increases: $20 + $2 x 14 = $48
   Price with -4 increases: $20 + $2 x (-4) = $12
   They will sell them for $48 or $12 each.

10. Let w be the width of the strip and A be the area of the unmown lawn.
    $A = (30 - 2w)(40 - 2w)$
    $A = 4w^2 - 140w + 1200$
    $4w^2 - 140w + 1200 = 30 \times 40 \div 2$
       $4w^2 - 140w + 600 = 0$
       $4(w^2 - 35w + 150) = 0$
         $4(w - 5)(w - 30) = 0$
    $w - 5 = 0$ or $w - 30 = 0$
         $w = 5$ $w = 30$ ← unreasonable width
    It is 5 m wide.

11. Its dimensions are 3 cm and 11 cm.

12. The integers are 17 and 19.

13. It reached the ground after 10 seconds.

14. The maximum height was 5.5 m.

15. Either $4.50 per kg or $5.50 per kg will generate $1237.50 in total.

16. The width of the lawn is about 18 m.

17. The dimensions are 12 cm and 16 cm.

18. Yes, it is possible. The integers are 7, 8, and 9.

Quiz 4

1. D   2. B   3. D   4. A
5. A   6. A   7. D   8. A

9. A: -1 and -3   10. $y = a(x + 3)(x - 5)$
   B: -1.5 $-2 = a(3 + 3)(3 - 5)$
   C: no x-intercepts $a = \dfrac{1}{6}$
   C ; A ; B $y = \dfrac{1}{6}(x + 3)(x - 5)$

11. $y = a(x + 5)(x - 2)$
    x-coordinate of vertex: $(-5 + 2) \div 2 = -1.5$
    y-coordinate of vertex: -49
    $-49 = a(-1.5 + 5)(-1.5 - 2)$
       $a = 4$
    $y = 4(x + 5)(x - 2)$
    $y = 4x^2 + 12x - 40$

Answers

12. $D = (-8)^2 - 4(1)(4) = 48$; 2 real roots
13. $D = 2^2 - 4(7)(10) = -276$; no real roots
14. $D = 2^2 - 4(-1)(-4) = -12$; no real roots
15. $D = (-12)^2 - 4(-3)(-12) = 0$; 1 real root
16. $(x - 8)(x + 3) = 0$ 17. $(3x - 5)(x - 3) = 0$
    $x-8 = 0$ or $x+3 = 0$ $3x-5 = 0$ or $x-3 = 0$
       $x = 8$ $x = -3$ $x = \dfrac{5}{3}$ $x = 3$
18. $(4x + 3)(x + 2) = 0$ 19. $2(3x^2 - 16x + 5) = 0$
    $4x+3 = 0$ or $x+2 = 0$ $2(3x - 1)(x - 5) = 0$
       $x = -\dfrac{3}{4}$ $x = -2$ $3x-1 = 0$ or $x-5 = 0$
                             $x = \dfrac{1}{3}$ $x = 5$

20. $x = \dfrac{-(-5) \pm \sqrt{(-5)^2 - 4(3)(2)}}{2(3)}$
    $x = \dfrac{5 \pm 1}{6}$
    $x = 1$ and $x \doteq 0.67$
21. $x = \dfrac{-(-9) \pm \sqrt{(-9)^2 - 4(4)(3)}}{2(4)}$
    $x = \dfrac{9 \pm \sqrt{33}}{8}$
    $x \doteq 1.84$ and $x \doteq 0.41$
22. $x = \dfrac{-(-17) \pm \sqrt{(-17)^2 - 4(7)(-40)}}{2(7)}$
    $x = \dfrac{17 \pm \sqrt{1409}}{14}$
    $x \doteq 3.90$ and $x \doteq -1.47$
23. $x = \dfrac{-(-2) \pm \sqrt{(-2)^2 - 4(-3)(5)}}{2(-3)}$
    $x = \dfrac{2 \pm 8}{-6}$
    $x \doteq -1.67$ and $x = 1$
24. $3(\frac{1}{3})^2 - 10(\frac{1}{3}) + 3 = 0$; a root
25. $4(\frac{3}{4})^2 + 11(\frac{3}{4}) - 3 = \dfrac{15}{2}$; not a root
26a. $-0.1d^2 + 1.1d + 0.5 = 0$
    $-0.1(d^2 - 11d - 5) = 0$
    $d = \dfrac{-(-11) \pm \sqrt{(-11)^2 - 4(1)(-5)}}{2(1)}$
    $d = \dfrac{11 \pm \sqrt{141}}{2}$
    $d \doteq 11.44$ or $d \doteq -0.44$ ← cannot be negative
    It was 11.44 m.
  b. $h = -0.1d^2 + 1.1d + 0.5$
    $h = -0.1(d^2 - 11d) + 0.5$
    $h = -0.1(d^2 - 11d + 30.25) + 3.025 + 0.5$
    $h = -0.1(d - 5.5)^2 + 3.525$
    The maximum height was 3.525 m.

27a. Let R be the revenue and x be the number of $0.25 decreases.
    $R = (4 - 0.25x)(6 + x)$
    $R = -0.25x^2 + 2.5x + 24$
    $-0.25x^2 + 2.5x + 24 = 28$
    $-0.25x^2 + 2.5x - 4 = 0$
    $-0.25(x^2 - 10x + 16) = 0$
    $-0.25(x - 2)(x - 8) = 0$
    $x - 2 = 0$ or $x - 8 = 0$
       $x = 2$ $x = 8$
    Price with 2 decreases: $4 - $0.25 x 2 = $3.50
    Price with 8 decreases: $4 - $0.25 x 8 = $2
    A sticker price of $3.50 or $2 will result in a revenue of $28 per customer.
  b. $R = -0.25x^2 + 2.5x + 24$
    $R = -0.25(x^2 - 10x) + 24$
    $R = -0.25(x^2 - 10x + 25) + 6.25 + 24$
    $R = -0.25(x - 5)^2 + 30.25$
    The maximum revenue is $30.25.
28. Let x be the length of the shortest side.
    $x^2 + (x + 2)^2 = (x + 4)^2$
    $x^2 + x^2 + 4x + 4 = x^2 + 8x + 16$
    $x^2 - 4x - 12 = 0$
    $(x - 6)(x + 2) = 0$
    $x - 6 = 0$ or $x + 2 = 0$
       $x = 6$ $x = -2$ ← cannot be negative
    $6 + 2 = 8$ and $6 + 4 = 10$
    The lengths are 6 cm, 8 cm, and 10 cm.
29. Let x be the smaller integer.
    $x^2 + (x + 6)^2 = 146$
    $2x^2 + 12x - 110 = 0$
    $2(x^2 + 6x - 55) = 0$
    $2(x - 5)(x + 11) = 0$
    $x - 5 = 0$ or $x + 11 = 0$
       $x = 5$ $x = -11$ ← cannot be negative
    $5 + 6 = 11$
    The integers are 5 and 11.
30. The value of the discriminant determines whether a quadratic equation has 0, 1, or 2 real roots. If the discriminant is less than 0, then there are no real roots. If the discriminant is 0, then there is one real root. If the discriminant is greater than 0, then there are two real roots.
31. If $ac < 0$, then the discriminant $b^2 - 4ac$ must be 0 or greater. This implies that real root(s) exist(s).

32. If $p(x-q)^2 + r = 0$ has 0 real roots, then $-p(x-q)^2 + r = 0$ has 2 real roots.
If $p(x-q)^2 + r = 0$ has 1 real root, then $-p(x-q)^2 + r = 0$ has 1 real root.
If $p(x-q)^2 + r = 0$ has 2 real roots, then $-p(x-q)^2 + r = 0$ has 0 real roots.

33a. $(-k)^2 - 4(k)(8) = 0$
$k^2 - 32k = 0$
$k(k - 32) = 0$
$k = 32$ or $k = 0$
↑
not applicable

b. $5^2 - 4(k)(k) = 0$
$25 - 4k^2 = 0$
$25 = 4k^2$
$k = \frac{\pm 5}{2}$
$k = -2.5$ or 2.5

34. $3x^2 - x + 8 = -x^2 + 4x + 7$
$4x^2 - 5x + 1 = 0$
$(4x - 1)(x - 1) = 0$
$4x - 1 = 0$ or $x - 1 = 0$
$x = 0.25$ $x = 1$
$3(0.25)^2 - 0.25 + 8 = 7.9375$
$3(1)^2 - 1 + 8 = 10$
There are two points of intersection: (0.25, 7.9375) and (1, 10).

Final Test

1. B   2. D   3. D   4. A
5. B   6. B   7. C   8. A
9. $= (x - 3)(x + 4)$
10. $= 3(x^2 + 4x + 4)$ 11. $= 8(4x^2 - 9)$
$= 3(x + 2)^2$ $= 8(2x - 3)(2x + 3)$
12. $y = a(x + 4)^2 + 7$ 13. $y = a(x - 5)(x + 3)$
$6 = a(0 + 4)^2 + 7$ $4 = a(-5 - 5)(-5 + 3)$
$a = -\frac{1}{16}$ $a = \frac{1}{5}$
$y = -\frac{1}{16}(x + 4)^2 + 7$ $y = \frac{1}{5}(x - 5)(x + 3)$
$y = -\frac{1}{16}(x^2 + 8x + 16) + 7$ $y = \frac{1}{5}(x^2 - 2x - 15)$
$y = -\frac{1}{16}x^2 - \frac{1}{2}x - 1 + 7$ $y = \frac{1}{5}x^2 - \frac{2}{5}x - 3$
$y = -\frac{1}{16}x^2 - \frac{1}{2}x + 6$
14. $y = a(x - 2)(x + 5)$ 15. $y = a(x - 2)^2 + 4$
$-5 = a(0 - 2)(0 + 5)$ $0 = a(3 - 2)^2 + 4$
$a = \frac{1}{2}$ $-4 = a$
$y = \frac{1}{2}(x - 2)(x + 5)$ $y = -4(x - 2)^2 + 4$
16. $y = 2(x^2 - 6x) + 7$
$y = 2(x^2 - 6x + 9 - 9) + 7$
$y = 2(x - 3)^2 - 11$
$(3, -11)$; $x = 3$; upward
17. $y = -3(x^2 - \frac{4}{3}x) - 1$
$y = -3(x^2 - \frac{4}{3}x + \frac{4}{9}) + \frac{4}{3} - 1$
$y = -3(x - \frac{2}{3})^2 + \frac{1}{3}$
$(\frac{2}{3}, \frac{1}{3})$; $x = \frac{2}{3}$; downward

18. $2x^2 - 4x - 70 = 0$ 19. $3x^2 + 11x - 4 = 0$
$2(x^2 - 2x - 35) = 0$ $(3x - 1)(x + 4) = 0$
$2(x - 7)(x + 5) = 0$ $3x - 1 = 0$ or $x + 4 = 0$
$x - 7 = 0$ or $x + 5 = 0$ $x = \frac{1}{3}$ $x = -4$
$x = 7$ $x = -5$
20. $y = 5(x^2 - 4x + 4) - 5$
$y = 5x^2 - 20x + 15$
$5x^2 - 20x + 15 = 0$
$5(x - 1)(x - 3) = 0$
$x - 1 = 0$ or $x - 3 = 0$
$x = 1$ $x = 3$
21. $x = \frac{-8 \pm \sqrt{8^2 - 4(3)(-3)}}{2(3)}$
$x = \frac{-8 \pm \sqrt{100}}{6}$
$x = \frac{-8 \pm 10}{6}$
$x \doteq 0.33$ and $x = -3$
22. $x^2 - 6x - 2 = 0$
$x = \frac{-(-6) \pm \sqrt{(-6)^2 - 4(1)(-2)}}{2(1)}$
$x = \frac{6 \pm \sqrt{44}}{2}$
$x \doteq 6.32$ and $x \doteq -0.32$
23. $8x^2 + 4x - 5 = 0$
$x = \frac{-4 \pm \sqrt{4^2 - 4(8)(-5)}}{2(8)}$
$x = \frac{-4 \pm \sqrt{176}}{16}$
$x \doteq 0.58$ and $x \doteq -1.08$
24. $D = 5^2 - 4(-4)(-1)$ 25. $D = (-12)^2 - 4(3)(12)$
$= 25 - 16$ $= 144 - 144$
$= 9$ $= 0$
2 real roots   1 real root
26. $\frac{1}{2}(x^2 + 2x - 15) + 10 = 0$ $D = 1^2 - 4(\frac{1}{2})(\frac{5}{2})$
$\frac{1}{2}x^2 + x - \frac{15}{2} + 10 = 0$ $= 1 - 5$
$\frac{1}{2}x^2 + x + \frac{5}{2} = 0$ $= -4$
no real roots
27. vertically stretched by a factor of 2, shift 3 units left and 2 units down
28. reflect in the x-axis, vertically stretched by a factor of 2, shifted 2 units right and 1 unit down
29. reflect in the x-axis, vertically compressed by a factor of $\frac{1}{4}$, shift 1 unit right and 1 unit up

$y = 2(x + 3)^2 - 2$
$y = x^2$
$y = -\frac{1}{4}(x - 1)^2 + 1$
$y = -2(x - 2)^2 - 1$

Answers

30. $h = 0.6t^2 - 3.6t + 20$
    $h = 0.6(t^2 - 6t) + 20$
    $h = 0.6(t^2 - 6t + 9 - 9) + 20$
    $h = 0.6(t - 3)^2 + 14.6$
    The minimum height was 14.6 m and he would be at this height after 3 seconds.

31a. Altitude at 0 s: $H = 5500 - (0)^2 = 5500$
    Altitude at 10 s: $H = 5500 - (10)^2 = 5400$
    Altitude fallen after 10 s:
    $5500 - 5400 = 100$
    The diver had fallen 100 m after 10 s.
  b. $5500 - t^2 = 1000$
    $-t^2 + 4500 = 0$
    $t^2 = 4500$
    $t = \pm\sqrt{4500}$
    $t \doteq 67$ and $t \doteq -67$ ← cannot be negative
    She was in freefall for 67 s.

32. Let w be the width of the rectangle.
    $w(3w + 4) = 20$
    $3w^2 + 4w = 20$
    $3w^2 + 4w - 20 = 0$
    $(w - 2)(3w + 10) = 0$
    $w - 2 = 0$ or $3w + 10 = 0$
    $w = 2$ $w \doteq -3.3$ ← cannot be negative
    $3(2) + 4 = 10$
    The dimensions are 2 cm and 10 cm.

33. Let x be the smallest number.
    $x^2 + (x + 2)^2 + (x + 4)^2 = 1331$
    $3x^2 + 12x - 1311 = 0$
    $3(x^2 + 4x - 437) = 0$
    $3(x - 19)(x + 23) = 0$
    $x - 19 = 0$ or $x + 23 = 0$
    $x = 19$ $x = -23$ ← not positive
    $19 + 2 = 21$ and $19 + 4 = 23$
    The numbers are 19, 21, and 23.

34. Let w be the width of the enclosure and A be the area.
    $A = w(\frac{1}{2}(320 - w))$
    $A = w(160 - \frac{1}{2}w)$
    $A = -\frac{1}{2}w^2 + 160w$
    $A = -\frac{1}{2}(w^2 - 320w)$
    $A = -\frac{1}{2}(w^2 - 320w + 160^2 - 160^2)$
    $A = -\frac{1}{2}(w - 160)^2 + 12\ 800$
    The maximum area is 12 800 m².

35. Let T be the income and x be the number of 10-cent increases.
    $T = (2 + 0.1x)(140\ 000 - 5000x)$
    $T = -500x^2 + 4000x + 280\ 000$
    $T = -500(x^2 - 8x) + 280\ 000$
    $T = -500(x^2 - 8x + 16) + 8000 + 280\ 000$
    $T = -500(x - 4)^2 + 288\ 000$
    Price after 4 increases: $2 + $0.10 × 4 = $2.40
    The maximum income will be generated at a price of $2.40.

36. A relation is linear if its first differences are constant. A relation is quadratic if its second differences are constant. If neither the first nor the second differences are constant, then the relation is neither linear nor quadratic.

37. To solve a quadratic equation, you may:
    - find the x-intercepts by graphing the parabola
    - represent the equation in standard form and apply the quadratic formula
    - factor the equation and find the roots

38. $y = 3x^2 - 18x + 29$
    $y = 3(x^2 - 6x) + 29$
    $y = 3(x^2 - 6x + 9) - 27 + 29$
    $y = 3(x - 3)^2 + 2$
    The new parabola with vertex at (-5,-10):
    $y = 3(x + 5)^2 - 10$
    $y = 3(x^2 + 10x + 25) - 10$
    $y = 3x^2 + 30x + 65$
    The equation is $y = 3x^2 + 30x + 65$.

39. Equation of the new graph:
    $y = -2(x - 1)^2 + k$
    $-14 = -2(-3 - 1)^2 + k$
    $k = 18$
    $y = -2(x - 1)^2 + 18$
    The translation from $y = -2(x + 8)^2 - 4$ to $y = -2(x - 1)^2 + 18$ is a shift of 9 units right and 22 units up.